Love Remembered in Summit County

SUMMIT COUNTY SERIES BOOK 6

KATHERINE KARROL

D1715174

This novel is a work of fiction. Names, characters, places, and incidents are either products of the author's imagination or used fictitiously. All characters are fictional, and any similarity to real persons, living or dead, is purely coincidental.

Cover Design by Ideal Book Covers

Background photo by Katherine Karrol

This book is dedicated to those who never give up on love.

The Summit County Series

The Summit County Series is a group of standalone books that can be read individually, but those who read all of them in order will get a little extra something out of them as they see the characters and stories they've read about previously continue and will get glimpses of characters that may be featured in future books. The series is set in a small county in northern Michigan where everyone knows everyone else, so the same characters and places make cameos and sometimes show up in significant roles in multiple books.

This series is near and dear to the author's heart because her favorite place in the world looks an awful lot like Summit County. She is certain that the people who know her and/or live in the area that inspired Summit County will think characters and situations are based on them or their neighbors (or even on her), and she assures them that they are not. The characters and stories are merely figments of her overly active imagination. Well, except for Jesus. He's totally real.

Chapter 1

CLAIRE'S HAND SHOOK AS she wiped a tear from her cheek. *Please be true.*

"Mrs. Millard?"

"Yes, I'm here . . . I'm sorry, Phil—could you repeat that?" This call seemed as unreal as the one she received a month ago.

"Of course." A smile carried through in the nurse's voice. "He's awake, and he's asking for you."

Thank You, Lord. It's real!

"Thank you." A sob escaped her lips. "I'm on my way. I'll be there as soon as possible."

As if in slow motion, Claire hit *End* on her phone and stared at the blank screen. She wanted to get up, but she was glued to her chair, her body too stunned to move.

Snap out of it, Claire! Quinn is awake!

Her limbs finally sprang into action. She jumped up from the kitchen table, knocking over her chair and almost spilling the half-empty cup of coffee on her morning devotion book. Wesley darted out from under the table, a blur of black and white as he sought refuge on the bookcase in the living room.

"Sorry to scare you, kitty-boy. He's awake!"

Her heart thudded in her ears as she ran to her bedroom to change out of her pajamas and into clothes. She grabbed the nearest sundress from her closet and pulled it over her head, neither noticing nor caring if it was wrinkled. Running back to the kitchen, she shoved her laptop, chargers, phone, and travel mug into her tote bag.

"He's awake! Gotta go!"

He's awake. He's asking for you.

Tears of relief streamed down her face. Throwing everything into the car, she thanked God over and over for giving her the news she'd been begging to hear for a month.

He's awake.

After getting into her car and turning on the ignition, the full reality of her situation hit her. Her thumping heart skidded to a halt.

Wait.

He's asking for me.

What does this mean?

"What do I do now, Lord? Why is he asking for me? As much as I've prayed for him to wake up, I should only feel happy about this and should be breaking land speed records to get to the hospital. I don't know how to move though. I don't know what to do." As horrible as it had been over the past month to see him in that hospital bed, at least she could be with him and take care of him. "What on earth do I say to him?"

She sat with her hands clutching the steering wheel, willing herself to put the car into gear and make the forty-five minute drive from home in Hideaway to the hospital in Traverse City.

"Lord, give me strength. I can't do it without You—and we both know how badly things turned out when I tried."

She sat there for another moment, staring at her white knuckles and trying to get her bearings. In a daze, she watched her next-door neighbor, Mr. Bradley, put red, white, and blue bunting on his porch railing. One would think the Fourth of July parade that was taking place in a few days was going to come down their street by the careful way he decked out his house. She watched him as thoughts of what would be waiting for her when she walked into Quinn's hospital room spun in her head.

Seeing his unconscious body with all the tubes, bandages, and monitoring equipment attached had become normal, as had the sounds and the smells of the intensive care unit. She knew the nurses by name, knew all the doctors' schedules, and knew what the numbers on the machines that surrounded his bed meant. The knowledge she was developing of head injuries and comatose states was approaching encyclopedic, and she had even been prepared to a certain degree for the upcoming stint in rehab and the possible need for him to re-learn to walk and talk.

She was as ready as she could be for what lay ahead for him physically. Still, she was completely unprepared to walk into that room, to look him in the eye.

The charade was about to end.

Chapter 2

QUINN KEPT HIS EYES closed and listened to the conversation the two nurses at his bedside were having about him. He hoped that as long as they assumed he was sleeping they would talk enough for him to learn something, but so far they'd only talked about his vital signs and coloring. None of their words were helping him piece together what was going on or why he was so banged up and in what could only be a hospital room.

His head hurt. Breathing hurt. Bones he didn't know existed hurt.

What he couldn't figure out, though, was why he was alone in the hospital room. *Where is Claire?*

His mind had started to veer toward the worst possible answer to his question, but finally one of the nurses gave him the answer he needed.

"Phil got ahold of his wife. She's on her way."

Why wasn't she already there? She must have had to step away just briefly, because there was no way that she would have left his side when he was lying in a hospital bed.

The nurses' conversation before they left the room didn't give him any clues about how he had gotten to what appeared to be an intensive care unit. He tried to remember what had happened, but the last thing he remembered was being with Claire at their new home.

They had been sitting on the deck that Claire's brother, Joe, and Quinn had finished a few hours earlier, looking at the colors of the September sunset. It was a fitting end to a long weekend of working on projects at the home they had moved into two weeks earlier. Joe was an architect, and he had designed the deck and helped Quinn build it with wood that Dad and Mom had given them as a housewarming gift. Claire and her mom, Sue, had cleaned up the garden and planted some shrubbery along the freshly-painted back fence, and it was starting to look like the sanctuary he and Claire had envisioned when they bought the place.

The day was perfect. It was the weekend after Labor Day, and with the temperatures starting to cool down and fall breeze picking up, it was a great work day. The only furniture they had for the deck so far was a rocking bench, and at the end of the day they sat side-by-side, polishing off their lemon custard ice cream from the stand by the grocery store.

Claire's eyes scanned the yard. "I still can't believe this is ours, Q. When we promised each other on our honeymoon that five years from then we would have our student loans paid off and would have a house where we could start our family, even I thought we were a little overconfident."

"Me too. But we did it! Living on Ramen noodles and not having cable was worth it, wasn't it?"

"It's everything I could have hoped for, and all that sacrifice was worth it." She looked back at the modest three-bedroom ranch as if it was the Taj Mahal. "I still can't believe we did it."

"You're right. We're amazing." He put his arm around her and kissed her on the cheek. "You're amazing. I love what you did with the yard."

She smiled as she rested her head on his shoulder. "Thank you, and you were right about putting the burning bush over there for fall color. This deck is definitely my favorite part of the house." Leaning into his embrace, she put her arms around him. "That might just be because you're here though."

"Are you saying I improve a room?"

"You improve everything." She leaned up and kissed the spot on his neck that she had always been partial to nuzzling, then snuggled closer. "So, the question is the same—where do you see us five years from right now?"

"My Claire, always the planner." He smiled and put his hands out toward the yard, forming brackets with his fingers as if setting up a video shot. "I see you sitting right where you are, round and pregnant and absolutely beautiful. And over there . . ." He gestured to the flat corner of the yard. "I see me helping our son and daughter make sandcastles together in the sandbox I built for them."

She stuck her lower lip out in a pouty frown. "Why don't I get to make sandcastles?"

He grinned and winked. "Because you're also holding the baby."

Her blue eyes became as round as saucers as she gasped and laughed. "Three kids and another on the way in five years?"

"We've always said we wanted them close together."

She giggled. "That's true. Hopefully the first one is already in there, and we can get this house filled with noise and smudges on the walls soon."

He leaned over and spoke into her flat belly. "Hey, are you in there, little boy or girl?"

"Okay, let's plan to be here in five years making sandcastles with our three and a half kids." She ran her fingers down his arm as she looked wistfully over at the sandcastle spot. "That's a great spot for a sandbox too. I'll even be able to watch the kids from the kitchen window when I'm washing bottles."

"And I'll wash the bottles while you make sandcastles too." He lowered his voice and leaned closer. "I'll also take the little monsters to their grandparents' houses so we can have some privacy to make more."

As he wiggled his eyebrows at her, she laughed. "It's a deal. We'll need to stay in practice so we can help God fill the house, after all."

"I like the way you think, Mrs. Millard." He took her hand and traced kisses along her fingers.

"You know our parents are going to fight over who gets to babysit, so your job of arranging babysitting should be pretty easy."

"I'll be highly motivated to be alone with you, so even if it's not easy, I'll convince them. I am in sales, after all."

Her blue eyes took on a serious look as she reached up and cupped his cheek. "Promise me we'll always have fun together and be here for each other, even when we have ten kids."

"I promise that too. Nothing could ever change what we have." He stroked her stomach as he mused, "I wonder if our firstborn is in there right now."

"I hope so."

Getting a mischievous look in her eye, she stood and reached her hand back to him.

He frowned. "Hey, where are you going?"

Her eyes twinkled as she bent forward and spoke in the flirty voice that she knew drove him wild. "We're going inside. These babies aren't going to make themselves, you know."

Giggling, she turned and ran into the house. "Catch me if you can!"

He bolted from the bench and chased her inside, catching up to her quickly in the hallway and pulling her into his arms. "I'm always gonna catch you."

"I'm always gonna let you." She wrapped her arms around his neck and pulled him close to whisper in his ear. "Always."

He pinned her to the freshly painted wall and planted a kiss on her that was intended to make her toes curl before lifting her and carrying her to their other favorite part of the house.

Quinn was pulled out of the memory when one of the nurses walked back into the room and adjusted something on one of the machines. Had something happened later that night that he didn't remember? He couldn't imagine what it could have been, but whatever it was broke him into pieces and put half of his body into a cast. It must have happened that night or early the next morning, because that was his most recent memory.

It was strange not to remember an accident, but maybe that was for the best. Claire would surely tell him all the details when she got there. She would make everything okay.

Chapter 3

CLAIRE FINALLY PUT THE car into gear and headed in the same direction she had driven every day for the last month. Would this be the last time?

"Lord, I know I asked you to do something big, but did You have to almost kill him and send him into a coma for a month? This isn't his fault."

She wiped another tear from her eye. "I'm sorry. I don't mean to tell You how to do Your job or anything. It just seems like You could have done something a little smaller."

She sighed as the knot took up its familiar place in her gut. "Well, the divorce is on hold now—or at least it was ten minutes ago, before he woke up." The tightness in her stomach made its way to her heart. "I'm going to need Your help to walk back into that hospital room. Help me to remember that no matter what happens, You are still on the throne and today I am still his wife. I will do whatever I can for him for as long as I can, and if he kicks me out, he kicks me out."

The nurse's words kept replaying in her mind as she made her way over the rolling hills that led through Summit County and toward the unknown. *Your husband is awake, and he's asking for you.* Phil didn't seem shocked that she had broken down in tears when he told her Quinn was awake. He probably heard tears like that pretty regularly working in an intensive care unit.

She was shaking by the time she finally pulled into the hospital parking lot, but she was comforted to see that her usual space was available. *I have a usual space in a hospital parking lot. That's something I never thought I would have.*

As much as she wanted Quinn to wake up and come back to health, part of her wished for one more day. It was easier walking into his room when he was in a coma. The thought of the man she loved so much looking past her and avoiding her again made her want to start the car back up and drive as far as she could get from that room.

Shaking the thought from her mind, she reminded herself that it didn't matter. At that moment she needed to be there with him, taking care of him, whether he wanted her there or not. At that moment she was still his wife.

She took one last deep breath and squared her shoulders. "Okay Lord, let's get this over with."

Chapter 4

QUINN STILL PRETENDED TO be asleep but very slowly opened his eyes a sliver, just enough to see the clock. Ten minutes had passed since they said someone talked to Claire. *How far is the cafeteria, anyway?*

Fifteen minutes ticked by. Then twenty. He could feel his breaths get shallow as he wondered where she could be.

Why wasn't she there? What could possibly be keeping her away? *Lord, please let her be okay. What would keep her from me when I'm lying in a hospital bed and she knows that I'm awake?*

As he lay there quietly, he tried to piece together how long he had been out of it or asleep or whatever he was. When he was eavesdropping on the nurses, he thought for sure that he had heard something about a coma. Had he actually been in a coma?

He tried to remember what happened before he woke up in the cold room hooked up to all the machines surrounding his bed, hearing all kinds of obnoxious beeping noises. His entire left side was in casts and in traction, and every little movement hurt. His body was broken, but he thanked God for being alive and for being able to wiggle his fingers and toes. At least he thought he was wiggling them.

But where is Claire? Lord, please don't let her be in another bed in this hospital.

The thought of her being hurt and in the state he was in sent his heart racing. One of the traitorous machines next to his bed started beeping frantically even while he tried to maintain his pretense of being asleep. The nurse walked in and stood in front of the machine for a moment, then shot something into the IV line.

No! I need to be awake!

Real sleep must have set in, because the next thing he knew, he felt Claire near him. He didn't have to open his eyes to know that it was her who was holding his hand. He would know her touch anywhere.

Chapter 5

CLAIRE FOUGHT TEARS AS she looked down on Quinn in the bed, so broken. She had gotten used to the casts and traction and bandages, but it still tore at her heart every time she saw him lying there like that. He didn't look at all like the strong, healthy thirty-three-year-old man he'd been a month ago.

They said that he had come out of the coma and was asking for her earlier, but lying there as he was, he looked almost the same as every other day since the accident. She wondered if he had slipped back into the coma or if he was just sleeping. Not knowing what to do or what was coming, she just watched him and prayed.

She sat close to his bed and held his hand, wondering if it was going to be the last time and thinking about how much she was going to miss being able to do something that was once so common and simple. Sitting at his side and holding his hand felt good, even considering the state he was in. When he woke up, everything might be just the same as it was thirty days ago, before the crash that almost killed him.

Leaning over him, she brushed a sandy brown lock of hair from his face. It had grown so much over the past month as he lay in his hospital bed, and it reminded her of what it looked like when they first met in their college

English class. As she tried to memorize every detail of his face, she couldn't help but feel like she was saying goodbye.

He looked so peaceful. When she brushed his hair away, his lips formed into a smile. She held her breath, fearing what would happen when he opened his eyes and willing him to keep them shut for just a moment longer. As he slowly opened his eyes, he looked into hers.

Instead of averting his gaze and avoiding eye contact with her as she'd become accustomed to, his smile grew. He looked at her the way he used to look at her, back before all the troubles started, and he tried to whisper her name.

She was frozen in place, unable to move, breathe, or think. Her heart raced, but all she could do was look back at him, fighting tears with every bit of strength she had.

What's happening? He was looking at her the way he used to—years ago, not a month ago.

Was it possible that something had changed in him?

Chapter 6

AHH, HERE SHE IS. And she's not in a wheelchair or a hospital gown. Thank You, Lord.

With her hand on his, he could feel the warmth flow up through his arm and straight into his heart. He wanted to say something to her, to wipe her tears away, but he didn't have the strength to speak or move. All he could do to communicate was squeeze her hand and try to tell her with his eyes that everything was going to be okay.

He felt so drugged. All he could do was study her. She looked different. She had changed her hairstyle again, for starters.

That must be it. Note to self: show no mercy when you tease her about going to the beauty shop while her husband was lying in the ICU.

His smile grew. *I'm gonna get a lot of mileage out of this one.*

He liked her new hair. The above-the-shoulder length would come in handy when he got out of the hospital and got back to kissing those shoulders and that neck. She had even colored it back to the natural deep brown that set off her blue eyes so perfectly. God had blatantly showed off His artistic skills when He created Claire.

As much as Quinn tried to wake up, his body resisted every step of the way. He wanted to hear her voice, especially to hear what had happened that got him to his broken state. It seemed that was going to have to wait, because his attempts to stay awake were no match for the heaviness that stretched from his limbs to his eyelids.

He tried to study her with the little energy he had despite her obvious discomfort with him doing so. Some things never changed.

Thankfully, she didn't look like she had a scratch on her. As long as she was okay, everything was going to be okay. He stopped fighting the heaviness in his eyes and let sleep take him.

Chapter 7

CLAIRE STAYED AT QUINN'S side for the rest of the morning, watching him and wondering when he would wake up again. She hadn't yet recovered from the way he had looked at her earlier, and she couldn't get the image out of her head. It was the old Quinn looking at her, the way he did before all the pain that life had inflicted on them and they had inflicted on each other.

Quinn's parents, Duane and Bev, walked into his room looking relieved and hopeful. Claire updated them on what the nurses had said and on what had happened—which was basically nothing—since she'd arrived. Since he was still asleep, she took the opportunity to take a short walk and get some air.

She stayed in the hallway that gave her a view of Quinn's door so she wouldn't miss a visit from any of the doctors, but it felt good to move her legs after sitting next to him like a statue looking for a sign that he would wake up again.

When she pulled out her phone and looked at the screen, she saw that she had twelve unread texts and a voicemail. The voicemail was from Mom saying she and Dad were on their way to the hospital and would be in the intensive care waiting room when she needed them. Claire looked at the time and knew that they were not there yet, with home being a forty-five minute drive for them too.

It came as a relief that part of her recent routine would remain the same now that Quinn was awake. Both her family and Quinn's had made daily visits to sit with him and support her over the month since the accident. They had worked out a schedule so that they weren't all there at the same time like they had been the first few days, staggering the visits to give Claire breaks and support through the day and to see Quinn without crowding the hospital room.

Most of the texts that had come in were from friends and family offering praise and prayers after hearing that Quinn was awake. Only having a few minutes, she resisted the urge to respond to all of them and instead called her sister, Brianna, to get an update on Quinn's business. He would probably ask about it as soon as he woke up, and she wanted to have an answer ready so that he would feel reassured.

As she waited for her to pick up, Claire thanked God again for Brianna. She was a recent MBA grad and had stepped in immediately after the accident to take over the majority of running the online business, which sold handmade gift items from local artists. With help from their sister-in-law, Emily, an accountant who had been doing some bookkeeping for Quinn, she had gotten a handle on it and had even started training Claire. Over the past week, Claire had been diligently studying the business and doing her part to keep it going so that it didn't all fall on Brianna.

The family didn't know about the marital rift or pending divorce, so they all assumed that Claire would be helping Quinn with it while he was recovering, and she went along to avoid raising questions. Learning the ins and outs of it gave her something to do during the long hours in the ICU and made her feel like she was still connected with him and able to do something for him. She hoped that knowing that the business was taken care of would help him to focus on the hard recovery he had ahead of him.

"Hey, sis!" Brianna's voice startled her from her musings.

"Brianna, I'm so sorry. I can only take a few minutes away. He's sleeping, but now that he's out of the coma, he could wake up any time."

"No problem. I didn't actually expect to hear from you today. How does he look?"

Claire thought of the loving way he had gazed at her earlier. It wasn't the time to go into that, and Brianna wouldn't understand why it had such a strong effect on her, so she opted for brevity. "He's slept most of the time I've been here and looks like every movement hurts. I was afraid they were going to try to push more heavy drugs on him, but they're sticking with sedating him for the moment."

"Well, that's a relief." The grin was obvious in Brianna's voice. "They're probably afraid of bringing up the topic of painkillers with you by this point, knowing that you're going to go all barracuda on them again."

Claire chuckled. "Yeah, there's probably a warning on his chart about me."

"Too bad." Brianna had a huge heart, but she was the most blunt person Claire knew. "You're being a good wife and carrying out his wishes. You must be beyond thrilled to have him back."

If only I had him back. "I'm thrilled that he's awake, and now we can focus on getting him better. He hasn't been able to talk or anything, so they're still assessing for brain damage. He did smile at me when he saw me." She couldn't stop her own smile from forming at the memory.

"Aww, that's so sweet. Even a coma couldn't stop your love."

She let out a laugh at Brianna's teasing. "Only you would find romance in an intensive care room, Brianna." Now that Brianna had reunited with her childhood sweetheart, she saw romance everywhere she looked.

"I can't help it. You two have always had sparks and the kind of marriage I want."

You wouldn't say that if you knew. She needed to change the subject. "How's the business today? I'm sorry I can't have a real lesson. I need to get back there in case he wakes up or another one of the doctors comes in."

"I understand, don't worry about it. I'll just keep doing what I'm doing, and we'll play it by ear. If you get time later, read the emails I included you on today. If you don't, it can wait."

"Okay. I'll be sure to check my email." Brianna shouldn't have to shoulder everything for so long.

"I keep telling you, I'll do this for as long as I need to. Quinn is your job right now. That is why you're on leave from your real job, you know."

"Yes, it is." Claire wished Brianna was there so she could hug her. If she didn't know her baby sister had grown up before, she sure did now. "Thanks again for all you're doing, sis. I don't know what I would do without you and all the time you've put in to figure it all out."

"I've got it covered. Give him a kiss and tell him I love him."

"I will."

"And I'll come up to see him tomorrow morning, okay?"

"He'll love it, and he'll be glad to know that you're taking care of everything for him. He has a lot of confidence in your business skills, you know." In the little time they had talked before the accident, he'd told her how impressed he was with the way Brianna was picking up on things.

"I'm just glad he and I had the time we had together before his accident so I could hear from him how everything worked." She blew out a breath. "I never would have imagined when he started teaching me to help me to get my own business started that I would be taking his over."

"You know he's going to appreciate it, and hopefully soon you can get back to your plans."

"Mine will hold until I'm done with his, and you can step back in whenever you're ready."

"Thanks. He'll relax, knowing you're at the helm." When Quinn started the company as a side hobby five years ago, he had shared all the details of the work with Claire, and they had done a lot of it together. They went to different art fairs every weekend and got to know the local artists and crafters, along with the latest trends. It was a fun project that they transformed from a hobby to a legitimate business, and they had hoped to build it enough that Claire could quit her job and they could work together. Well before the time of the accident, spending time together had become excruciating and the marriage was over. The growing company had slowly become all his, and she kept all of her focus on her own new job as the administrator of a preschool.

Her steps were heavy as she walked back to Quinn's room and prepared to once again act the part of the wife who would be sticking by her husband's side for the long haul. Duane and Bev stayed with her and together they all watched him sleep, as they had so many times over the last month.

After convincing both sets of parents to go down to the cafeteria for dinner, Claire stayed with Quinn. She was snacking on cheese and crackers when Dr. Corbin, the neurologist who reminded her of Grandpa Callahan, walked in with his usual smile.

"How is our patient doing this evening?"

"He looks the same to me. He woke up once, smiled at me, and went back to sleep, but that was hours ago."

The man nodded, his gaze swaying between Quinn and the record in his hand. "Well, he's still pretty heavily sedated, so I wouldn't expect anything much different than that. His vitals are all strong, and if he continues as he has, we'll look at weaning him from the oxygen tonight."

"So soon? That's wonderful new—" A movement caught Claire's eye and she turned to see Quinn stirring.

Dr. Corbin saw it too and stepped close to his bedside. "Good afternoon. My name is Dr. Corbin. Can you tell me yours?"

Claire reflexively reached for her necklace and began fingering the cross. Quinn's last gift to her had been a great source of comfort during the month she had watched him fight for his life.

"Quinn Millard." Despite how raspy it sounded, hearing his voice for the first time in a month made Claire's heart leap and brought tears to her eyes. She hadn't realized until that moment just how much she had missed hearing it. His hoarseness made it hard to hear, but it was clear that he was giving the right answer. She hoped that was a good sign as the doctor assessed for brain damage.

"It's nice to officially meet you, Quinn. Do you know where you are?"

"Hospital." He winced. The nurses had warned that his throat would be raw from all the time he'd spent on a ventilator. It had only been out for a week, so it wasn't a surprise.

"How about what state we're in?"

"Michigan."

"Good. Do you remember what happened that got you here with us?"

"No." A look of panic flashed across Quinn's face, and he looked to Claire and reached for her hand. He looked so childlike, so vulnerable.

She held his gaze as she took his hand and gave it a reassuring squeeze. It was probably best that he didn't remember the terrifying moment that he stared death in the face or the time it took for the fire department to get him out of the car.

"How old are you, Quinn?"

"Twenty-eight."

Every cell in Claire's body jolted when the wrong answer came out of his mouth.

She and Dr. Corbin exchanged a look. Quinn had always been a practical joker, but he looked just as serious as he had when he said that he was in the hospital and when he said his name.

He must have just misspoken.

The doctor didn't miss a beat and continued his questioning.

"Can you tell me who this lady is sitting next to your bed?"

Quinn smiled and turned his hazel eyes back to her. "My Claire."

A fresh batch of tears found its way up from deep inside her. She didn't remember the last time he had called her that.

"What do you do for a living, Quinn?"

"Sell cars . . . dad's dealership."

A shock tore through Claire. Her breath caught, and she had to fight to stay calm.

Not misspeaking. What's going on?

Dr. Corbin continued with his questioning as if nothing was amiss, even though Claire was sure he saw her reaction. When he had gotten enough answers, he patted Quinn's good foot. "I'll let you get some sleep now. You've had some serious injuries and your body is still recovering, so I don't want to wear you out with conversation. I'm even going to send your wife home for the night in a little while so that you can sleep."

Claire followed him into the hallway and closed Quinn's door. Dr. Corbin turned to her as they made their way toward the nurses' station.

"The car dealership?"

"He left it after his own business took off three years ago."

"That explains why you went white as a sheet." He set his tablet on the counter.

Claire followed the motion in a daze, but tried to focus on his words.

"I had hoped that the age answer was an anomaly, but it appears that's not the case. We'll keep an eye on it for a couple of days and see what happens. We never know how long amnesia will last, but for now, don't say anything to try to bring him into the present." He patted her arm as if to accentuate his directive. "His health is too precarious right now to withstand more trauma, and it would be a shock to his system."

"Amnesia?" She knew it sounded like a stupid question, given that she heard what Quinn said, but she was incredulous.

No wonder he's being so loving. He doesn't remember how he really feels.

"Yes, sometimes it happens after head injuries and lengthy comas. He's had both, so it's not a surprise."

She nodded. "I guess not."

"Sometimes people with retrograde amnesia—that's amnesia for past events—come back to regain all of their memories the next day, and sometimes it takes months."

"Months?"

"Most people regain their memories at some point, but there are no guarantees." Despite the terrifying words he was saying, his voice remained calm and reassuring. "A month in a coma can do a lot of damage to a memory above and beyond what the head injury already did. Now that he's awake, we'll assess his ability to keep new information. He tracked well in the short conversation, which is a good sign, but we'll keep assessing. We'll learn more over the next few days."

She stared at the floor in stunned silence with one arm tightly around her waist and the other hand on her necklace as she tried to grasp what it all meant.

"I know this is a lot to take in. We'll talk more tomorrow when I'm back for morning rounds. I want you to go home soon and get some sleep, because now is the time when he's really going to need you. It's clear from the way he looks at you that you're his strength right now, and what he needs most from you is to give him comfort and reassurance."

He motioned to one of the nurses and looked at Claire intently. "Remember, as much as you might want to, don't try to get him back to the present. I've learned over the years to be extra cautious with this sort of thing, so just to be sure that no well-meaning family members try to stir his memory or say something accidentally, I'm going to put a halt on his visitors for the time being. You're the only one I want in that room with him."

Thankfully, one of the nurses called him before he could see her panic rise. How was she supposed to act with Quinn if he didn't remember?

Chapter 8

QUINN WAS GETTING GOOD at opening his eyes just a sliver and seeing what was going on around him without the nurses noticing.

It reminded him of when he and his brother used to pretend they were asleep as kids on Christmas Eve. Evan always got caught because he couldn't help squinting, but Quinn had learned how to keep the rest of his face still. If it wouldn't give him away or hurt so much, he would have laughed about how one of the silly things he did as a child trying to fool both his parents and Santa Claus was helping him as an adult trying to gather information.

He strained to hear what the nurses were saying. They stepped into the hallway, and he couldn't make out the muffled words. He turned his head a bit, careful to do it slowly to reduce the chances of the hammer-like pounding in his head. No one had to tell him he had a nasty head injury. The pounding let him know that piece of news with even the smallest movement.

His ribs hurt with every breath, and the casts and traction equipment made moving nearly impossible. Even if it was probably best that he didn't remember what happened, it was also unsettling. Whatever got him into that hospital almost took his life.

Guessing that it must have been a car accident either later in the night he remembered or early the next day, he hoped that he had been alone. Claire didn't look injured, although she looked extremely thin. He missed her full cheeks and sweet smile and wondered if she had stopped eating because she was keeping vigil at his bedside. It was also possible that she was pregnant and morning sickness was taking a toll on her. If that was the case, he would insist on her visiting him less and resting more.

Being at the hospital was obviously wearing on her. She had looked so tense yesterday, like it was taking everything she had to be strong. She even looked a little bit older. Maybe that part was hospital lighting.

When she walked into the room, she wore the look of tension again. It was almost as if she was afraid of what might happen next.

He kept his eyes only open a sliver so he could study her. The tiny worry crease next to her eyebrow was deep as she approached him and tucked the blankets around him. How many times had she done that for him? And just how long had he been in a hospital bed if she looked so comfortable doing so?

It was strange having her tend to him as she was. She had always taken good care of him on the rare occasion that he was sick, but she had never had to maneuver around a feeding tube, oxygen tube, or an IV line. One would have thought she was a nurse, the way she worked around every-thing, not a preschool teacher.

He realized as he snuck peeks at her that he must have been there for quite some time for her to become so adept at working around the equip-ment and for her to lose most of the tan she'd gotten during the summer. The amount of time that had passed was just one of the things he would ask her when he had the energy and it didn't hurt so much to talk.

When he got a whiff of what was in the cup she had set on his bed table, his heart fell. That was the answer he didn't want about the possibility of morning sickness. She had sworn off coffee when they started trying to have a family, and if she was pregnant, she wouldn't have started it up again.

How long have I been like this?

Chapter 9

CLAIRE WAS THANKFUL FOR good, strong coffee as she adjusted the blankets that had shifted from their position. She had barely gotten any sleep, thanks to her mind spinning in every direction, and this would be the first of some very long days if she was the only person allowed in the room with Quinn.

Sharing visiting times with their families over the month he'd been there had helped, but even then being at the hospital all day had tired her out. They were all disappointed that they couldn't see him now that he was awake and he had lost five years, but both sets of parents had decided that they would continue to spend time in the waiting room each day in case she wanted to have company there while he slept.

As had become her daily habit, she noted the numbers on each of the screens. Now that he might regain his memory and retreat from her at any time, that was easier than looking directly at him. It was exhausting to wonder if or when he would regain his memory and what he would be like then. The only way she was going to be able to get through it was to set aside thoughts of the future and take each second as it came.

He had looked like he was sleeping when she walked in, and she had carefully adjusted the bedding around him. Needing something to do, she straightened the corner of the blanket. When she looked at his face, he broke into a smile again. She couldn't help but meet it.

"You've been pretending to sleep, haven't you?"

He grunted as he attempted to laugh. She knew his tricks well and was glad to see that his sense of humor was intact. It was like medicine to her soul to share a smile with him. It had been way too long.

She took a step closer. "Very sneaky. Remind me to tell the nurses not to talk about you in front of you." That was exactly what she needed to tell them. "Are you comfortable?"

He gave her a look that said, "Are you kidding?"

"How about as comfortable as a man in traction can be?"

He attempted to smile and slowly nodded.

When she stood next to his bed, he tried to say something to her, but she didn't understand. The nurses had said that it would take a while for his voice to return to normal. She leaned in and asked him to say it again.

"What . . . happened?"

"You were in a car accident. Someone driving a delivery truck crossed the center line and hit you." *Because it was so important that he read a text message.* Quinn didn't need to know the details that made her anger surge, so she kept her answer simple.

"You too?"

"No, I wasn't with you. You were alone in the car."

He half-smiled, seemingly pleased that she hadn't been hurt. The door opened, and Claire was glad to have a reason to stop talking more about the accident.

As promised, Dr. Corbin had come to check on him while on his morning rounds. "Good morning. The nurses tell me you had a good night and got some sleep. Do you mind if I do some poking to see how your nervous system is recovering?"

Quinn raised his eyebrows and shrugged.

"I think he means you can go ahead."

"You've got a good translator here, Quinn." He pulled out something that looked like a pen or a laser pointer. "I've told your wife that I don't want you to have any visitors but her for a couple of days so that you can continue to get rest."

Quinn looked at her and smiled as he tried to nod his approval.

Yup, Doc, he's still got amnesia.

Quinn flinched and winced as Dr. Corbin poked his arms, hands, legs, and feet.

"I'm sorry, I know this isn't pleasant, but this is a very good sign. Can you push against my hand with your foot? Good." He moved back to Quinn's arm. "How about here?"

Claire breathed a prayer of thanks as she watched him follow the doctor's instructions. She had felt him squeeze her hand, but it was a relief to have someone who knew what they were looking for assess it and see progress.

"This is exactly what we want to see." Dr. Corbin smiled at Quinn. "I'm pleased to tell you that we can rule out paralysis and major nerve damage. You will need physical and occupational therapy to get those muscles back in line, but it all starts with the nerves. We're going to continue weaning you off the oxygen, and soon you'll be able to try to swallow more than just clear liquids."

Quinn gave a weak thumbs-up.

"We're still going to keep you somewhat sedated to help with the pain and sleep."

Claire tried not to show her relief. Now that he was out of the coma and didn't know what year it was or that they were technically separated, she had no idea how she was going to pass the time with him during his waking moments. It wasn't as if she could catch him up on current events or they could talk about the things they used to talk about. The few conversations they'd had over the last several months were not any that she would like to repeat, and it felt as if they'd completely forgotten how much they used to enjoy each other.

The last big conversation before the accident was about how they would divide up their assets in the divorce. Quinn had insisted on being extremely generous and making sure that any financial hardship fell on him despite Claire's attempts to divide their assets evenly. Claire shivered as she remembered the businesslike manner with which they had sat together with paper, pens, and calculators. Taking amicable to a new level didn't make talk of severing the life they had built together any less heart-wrenching.

Fortunately, she had bought the latest John Grisham novel in the hospital gift shop on her way up to his room. Reading it to him when he was awake would go a long way in avoiding too many questions about real life. It would also help her to avoid the temptation of believing that the way he was acting toward her was permanent. Or real.

Chapter 10

QUINN DIDN'T WANT TO waste his limited energy when Claire wasn't there, so he lay quietly in his bed while he waited for her to arrive.

The last few days had gone by quickly. He spent most of his time sleeping, and when he was awake, Claire read to him. She didn't seem to mind. As she read the book, she looked more like her relaxed self and less like the tense woman who had been at his bedside since this all started. Her years spent reading to her preschool classroom had built great skills for reading aloud, and she somehow even managed to completely avoid slipping into a voice used for reading to children while she read the legal thriller.

It was helpful to listen to the books, too, because trying to communicate was painful and exhausting. His throat was sore from being on a ventilator at some point after his accident, and it took every ounce of strength to squeeze even a few hoarse words out. The doctors had promised that his throat and vocal cords would improve with rest, and he hoped it would happen soon.

The physical therapist had already started some basic movement and stretching exercises and seemed to want to get him up and around as soon as he could. Quinn wished he could speed along the timeline until he could stay awake long enough to have a real conversation with Claire. She looked so different sitting at his bedside, and it wasn't just the haircut or weight loss. Her brow was almost constantly furrowed with worry, especially when she walked into the room in the mornings and when he woke up from a nap. It was as if she expected something terrible to happen. He'd tried to reassure her with his eyes and with the few words he had the strength to form, but it didn't seem to be enough.

He prayed while he waited for her to arrive. *If there is a way to take away her fears, please do it. I haven't found it yet, but I'm listening for any direction You can give me.*

She walked into the room with what had become her usual fearful look, and he tried to give her an optimistic smile as he reached out to her with his good hand. Her brow unfurled and she smiled as she took his hand and squeezed it. As she leaned over to give him a kiss on the forehead, he used all of his strength to pull and hold her near. Without letting go of her hand, he gazed at her and pointed to his cheek. She obliged with a kiss there too.

As she stood back up, she turned away quickly, but not before he saw her wipe a tear from her eye.

Since when does giving me a kiss make her cry? Why does she look terrified every time she walks into my room?

Something is very wrong here.

The tension he saw in her even seemed to be affecting his dreams. He kept having dreams where he saw her crying and turning away from him when he tried to comfort her. He'd even had one where he was crying alone in a car and she was nowhere to be found. Even though they were only dreams, they made him shudder and wake up with a heaviness in his chest. If the tension was bad enough to affect his dreams, he needed to find out what was going on.

It hurt when he tried to ask the question, so he motioned with his hand to simulate writing.

"Do you want to write something?"

He nodded, and she looked around the room and in her purse. Finding nothing, she went into the hallway to ask at the nursing station. When she returned, she had a small whiteboard in her hand and a look of victory on her face. She carefully and slowly adjusted his bed so that he could be in a more comfortable position and propped pillows under his arm, then moved the chair closer so she could hold the board for him.

Straining, he wrote, I LOVE YOU.

Her eyes filled with tears, and she swallowed hard.

"I love you too, Quinn." More tears.

Time to jump in. AM I WORSE THAN I FEEL?

She looked confused when she shook her head. "The doctors say you're doing great. You've heard them. That's why you're moving to the step-down unit soon, maybe even in a couple of days."

He motioned for her to erase the board. She complied, then looked with anticipation as he began writing again. Writing what he had took more strength than he thought it would, but he was determined to have a conversation.

WHY CRY WHEN YOU SEE ME? AFRAID I'LL DIE?

This time a tear spilled down her cheek when she shook her head.

"You're out of the woods and not going to die. This has been scary and hard, and I'm just emotional." She stroked his arm. "All I want is for you to be okay. You're getting better every day, and I'm crying happy tears."

Bull.

She wasn't telling him the whole truth. They had been inseparable since they met as sophomores in college, and the years they had spent together had made them experts on each other. He knew what her happy tears looked like, and while he did see those occasionally from the hospital bed, the majority of what he saw when she got tears in her eyes was fear and sadness.

Writing and getting nowhere had exhausted and frustrated him as much as speaking did, so he pushed the board back toward her.

"Tired."

"Okay. We can do more later if you want. Do you want me to read to you or would you rather sleep?"

"Sleep."

And plot. And listen. I need to figure out what is going on around here.

He had always loved a good mystery in a book, but living it in real life with himself as the protagonist was for the birds.

Chapter 11

CLAIRE PACED AS SHE waited for Dr. Corbin to make his rounds. Quinn had been awake for five days, and she hoped the time for avoiding the conversation about his amnesia could be coming to a close. His frustration at her vague answers was obvious, and she could tell he didn't believe her. It was ironic that the man who had become a virtual stranger to her over the last year had reverted to the one who knew her so well he practically lived inside her head.

She didn't want him to think there was something medically wrong that they were holding back and didn't want to do anything to cause him further stress. She also didn't want to give him something else to be mad at her about when he regained his full memory. He had always denied holding anger toward her, but she couldn't come up with a better explanation for his distance.

When Dr. Corbin approached her, she asked if they could talk in an office in case Quinn wasn't really sleeping and was trying to eavesdrop. It wasn't easy to hear what was being said outside his room, but given his skill at appearing to sleep while listening in and his sharp senses, she wasn't about to take any chances. The doctor led her through a door into the small break room and gestured for her to sit at the table, then sat across from her.

"You look troubled, Mrs. Millard. Has something changed?"

"He knows something is wrong. I've been doing what you said to do and he doesn't know the year or anything about the amnesia, but he can practically read my mind." She laced her fingers together under the table to stop herself from fidgeting. "Despite my best attempts, he knows I'm keeping something from him and he's asking questions."

He nodded along as she spoke, almost smiling. "Well, that's quite a coincidence, because I was planning to talk to you about this today and tell you that it's time to tell him. He's almost ready to go to the step-down unit, but I'd like to tell him about the amnesia while he's still here and being closely monitored."

Thank You, Lord. I think. "Okay. Is there a best way to tell him?"

It was a relief that she didn't have to lie to Quinn anymore, but she dreaded the questions he would be asking once he knew. Hopefully Dr. Corbin wouldn't make her tell him everything right away. If he gave her some time, she could frame the answers to Quinn's questions very carefully.

Dr. Corbin's confident demeanor reassured her and calmed her nerves. "I'll explain everything to him with you there. I know this goes without saying, but remember that I don't want you to fill him in on five years of details today." He stood and pushed his chair back to the table. "As a matter of fact, I would prefer that you hold off so he can remember as much as possible on his own. The more he remembers, rather than being told, the more the memories will take hold and expand. Stick to the basics and to his questions so we don't overwhelm him with this."

Relief unwound some of her muscles. "Okay."

He paused with his hand on the doorknob. "Ready?"

"Yes. Let's get this over with." *Lord, please give us the words, and help Quinn to handle this news. Please don't let it shake him so much that it sends him backward. And please give me wisdom as I answer the inevitable questions.*

As they entered Quinn's room together, she took a deep breath and gripped God's peace. When she pictured herself as the woman touching Jesus's garment and being healed, His warmth flowed around her. *Thank You, Lord. I feel You here. Please let Quinn feel You too.*

Chapter 12

QUINN STARED AT DR. Corbin, then Claire, waiting for the punchline. Claire squeezed his hand again and gave him a sympathetic smile.

No. Can't be. Impossible.

Amnesia?

Dr. Corbin told him the date then wrote it next to the day of the week and the name of the nurse on duty on the large whiteboard on the wall.

July? It was just September.

The machine next to his bed started beeping, and he recognized it as the one that measured his heart rate. When Claire stroked his hand, the beeping quieted.

"July?" He thought he had only imagined the sound of fireworks last night. That wasn't his imagination; it was a holiday celebration.

When he searched her eyes, she nodded.

"Five years?"

She nodded again, and her tears looked ready to spill over.

Questions flew through his mind like a fastball. *What did I miss? How many children do we have? She's here every day. Are the kids wondering where Mommy and Daddy are? Is this why I haven't had visitors? Are our families taking turns babysitting? Are they even all still alive?*

The beeping ramped up again. The nurse approached his IV line with a needle in hand, looking to Dr. Corbin for direction to proceed.

Quinn pleaded with her with his eyes. He needed to be awake.

Dr. Corbin patted his hand, pulling his attention away from the nurse. "Quinn, we're going to give you something to help you sleep right now so this news doesn't set you back." He had a tone of compassion and finality. "You're doing great, and we'll talk more in a few hours."

As he signaled the nurse to inject the medicine into the IV line, Quinn shook his head, trying to stop them. The movement made his throat feel like it was going through a meat grinder, but he didn't care.

He wanted answers, not sleep. And he wanted the beeping machine to stop.

When he woke up, he looked for Claire. She was on the other side of the room with her legs stretched out on the spare chair, concentrating on something on her computer. The puckered look on her face reminded him of what she looked like in college when she was preparing for finals, and he stayed still for a moment, enjoying the opportunity to watch her. When she glanced over and saw that he was awake, she closed the computer and moved her chair back to his bedside. There was that worried look again.

He wrote in the air again to ask for the whiteboard so he could tell her about the strange dream he'd had right before he woke up. The doctor had said he had amnesia and had lost five years of time. That dream had left him feeling as unsettled as the dreams about the two of them crying alone and rejecting each other's attempts at comfort.

As he watched her reach for the small board and marker, the large board on the wall at the foot of his bed caught his eye. Each day they wrote the day of the week and name of the nurse on duty on the top, but now it had the date too.

Just like in the dre—it wasn't a dream!

His body jerked, and he looked at Claire, wide-eyed. She looked at the wall and back at him as she brought the small board over to him, her face filled with concern. "Are you okay?"

He scribbled quickly and barely legibly. DATE

She looked at the whiteboard, then pulled her phone out of her pocket to show him the home screen. It showed the same date as the board in front of him.

"Amnesia?" He winced at the burning in his throat.

Claire nodded slowly. "You remember what Dr. Corbin told you?"

Why did his throat have to hurt so much? If he wasn't desperate to speak before, he sure would be now. He needed answers, and since no one was offering many, the only way to get them was to ask a lot of questions.

Everything that had been so confusing was starting to make sense. Claire's hair . . . weight . . . the unfamiliar clothes she was wearing and the new cross necklace. . . .

Five years.

The pen sat still in his hand as he stared at the whiteboard. *Where do I even start?*

He wrote slowly so she would be able to read it. WHAT HAVE I MISSED?

Her brow furrowed, then her lips curved into a smile. "The Cougars finally got to the World Series."

His heart started to soar, then she added. "They didn't win, but they got there."

He shook his head. *Stupid Cougs still know how to break my heart.*

Claire pulled the chair close and sat back down.

She's not telling me important stuff. He looked at her expectantly, waiting for more.

She placed her hand back on his. "I know you have questions, and I promise I'll tell you everything you need to know in time. Dr. Corbin is hoping your memory will come back naturally and doesn't want me to flood you with information." When he frowned, she gave him a compassionate smile. "He said it will be better for you to remember more and for the memories to make sense to you if most of them come back on their own."

He nodded, unsatisfied with the plan.

"What is the last thing you remember?"

NEW HOUSE

DECK

SANDCASTLE

His chest filled with warmth as he remembered making their new house a home and dreaming together about what the future held for them. His smile grew so big at the memories that it hurt, then his thoughts returned to the first question he had when he found out how much time he'd lost. Had they started their family there, like they had hoped to? Was the little blonde girl with the princess crown from the tea parties in his dreams their daughter?

"Kids?"

Claire took in a sharp breath. Tears filled her eyes again as she shook her head.

Five years? And no kids?

Her voice was quiet as she choked out the words. "We were never able to conceive."

"Oh, Claire." Pushing the board away, he stretched his arm toward her. When she leaned over him and carefully hugged him, he held onto her with the little bit of strength he had. It didn't matter that it was making his broken ribs hurt more or that it might disturb the feeding tube and wires attached to his chest. He didn't care about any of that. His tears mingled with Claire's on his neck as they held each other and cried together.

He didn't want to ask any more questions. That was more than enough painful information for one day.

No wonder Claire looked so sad and fearful. It had to be awful for her to wonder if he remembered and worse to think of having to be the one to tell him.

Had they messed something up when they decided to put off having children during the first five years they were married? They had both wanted them immediately, but after watching others struggle with finances, they decided they would pay off their student loan debts and buy a house before starting their family. Getting married right out of college, they thought they had all the time in the world.

People said they were crazy because of the extremes they went to in order to pay off their loans so quickly, but they had made it into a challenge and an adventure. Every time one of them got sick of watching the same DVDs over and over or living in a cramped one-bedroom apartment, the other reminded them that it was for their future family.

They had made their last student loan payments two months before their first mortgage payment. When they had figured out how to manage the house financially, they took it as a sign that God had a plan to create their first baby there and were determined to help Him out by doing their part. The day they moved into the house, they made an event of throwing away their birth control and celebrated with the first of many tries to make a baby. Creating both their home and their family at the same time was exciting, and they had high hopes for their future. Had they offended God by planning too much?

When Claire left his hospital room that evening, Quinn tried to remember every detail of that time, hoping it would stir his memory. Exhausted, he fell asleep as he was picturing the day he had spent making the kitchen over by repainting the cupboards and replacing all the knobs and fixtures.

Maybe remembering those mundane details would lead to more significant ones. He could only hope.

Chapter 13

CLAIRE GRIPPED THE STEERING wheel and stared at the bush in front of her parking space. She wasn't sure which was worse, not telling Quinn that he had lost time, or having to tell him the most painful thing that he didn't remember.

Actually, the fact that they didn't have children wasn't the most painful thing. She dreaded telling him that it had started a series of hurts that ended with them in a divorce attorney's office.

She squeezed her eyes shut. It was ironic that the last memories he had were of getting settled into the home they had been preparing to put on the market when he had his accident. Those early days of unpacking boxes, painting, and doing deep cleaning and repairs had been exhausting, but they were full of laughter and hope. The more recent ones spent packing boxes, decluttering in preparation for the real estate agent, and making upgrades for someone else to enjoy were full of only tears and despair. The neatly-stacked boxes in the garage were nothing more than a tangible reminder of broken dreams and a dead marriage.

After Quinn had conjured up the image of making the sandcastles with their children, he had commissioned one of the local artists he eventually worked with to make a miniature sandcastle figurine for Claire as a reminder of what was to come. That figurine had comforted her in the months that followed when no pregnancy came to be. When those months turned into a year, then another, and she and Quinn grew further apart, she had stuffed the figurine into the back of a drawer where she wouldn't have to see it and be reminded that sometimes dreams turn into heartbreak. It was easier dealing with the bad times if she didn't have the comparison to the good times. Or so she thought.

As a tear escaped her eye with no one around to see it, she thanked God for having her car to escape to when Quinn slept. Having a place where she could cry and pray was one of the few things keeping her sane. She had even snuck out there on occasion when her parents were on the premises when she needed the alone time. It was easy to let them assume the tears were about his condition when he was still in danger and in the coma, but now that he was on the mend, it would only raise questions that she was not going to answer.

As she blew her nose and wiped her eyes for what must have been the fortieth time, she looked up and saw her in-laws pull into the parking lot. They waved at her and found a spot near hers.

Now that Quinn was awake and aware of the situation, Dr. Corbin had given the okay for them to visit him. They had been very patient and understanding, but she knew it was killing them to not be able to see him over the past five days.

Her family wanted to see him, too, but since he was still in the ICU for at least the rest of the day and Dr. Corbin wanted to be cautious, Duane and Bev were the only ones allowed. It helped that the many people who couldn't visit were praying, and she could feel those prayers keeping her upright.

Claire tried to hold back her tears as she got out of her car and met up with them in the parking lot. Both she and Quinn had grown up in families that didn't show a lot of emotion. Her family had changed when they went through both the devastation of losing her sister-in-law, Janie, and the joy of her niece, Lily, entering the family over three years ago, but his was still as reserved as always. Duane and Bev were kind, loving people, but they avoided strong feelings like the plague.

She and Quinn had tried to fight against such family models in their own marriage and had done well with being open and expressive with each other until the pain became so great that they reverted to old patterns of holding in their feelings and affection. Once they slipped into the old ways both with each other and with God, the end seemed inevitable. They both turned in to themselves and away from everyone else—including each other, eventually. That was when the loneliest time of her life began. Their isolation was so complete that apart from the divorce attorney, there was not a single soul who knew what was going on in their marriage.

Shoving her thoughts aside, she began filling Duane and Bev in on Quinn's condition as they walked into the hospital together. They handled medical facts like pros, but they were as rocked by the amnesia as she was.

"He really doesn't remember anything? Even after you told him about the amnesia?"

Claire held her chuckle as she imagined Quinn's response to Bev's question. "Not a thing. The last thing he remembers is building the deck on the house after we moved in."

"And the doctor doesn't think we should help him along?"

Claire shook her head, perhaps more forcefully than she should have. "No, he's absolutely forbidden it. He said it will be much better for Quinn to remember things on his own. So he doesn't know about your new condo or your dog or our cat." She started to get nervous, wondering if it would be possible for Bev to avoid talking about the animals. The woman could go on for days about the cute things her precocious puppy did.

Duane jumped in. "And he doesn't know about leaving the dealership. What do I say if he asks about work?"

This was going to be harder than she thought. "You can tell him that there's plenty of time to talk about that when he gets well and remind him that we're not supposed to tell him things. That's what I've done when he's asked questions. He knows we're supposed to let him remember on his own, so he's been pretty good about not asking too much."

Duane exhaled but fidgeted with his Cougars baseball cap. She put her hand on his arm and smiled at him. "I did tell him about the Cougs getting to the Series."

He shook his head. "He's going to be glad he doesn't remember the Series."

They walked slowly, and Claire was thankful that Dr. Corbin had said he wanted their visit to be brief. She was already in knots hoping they didn't slip up or say the wrong thing.

"Another thing you should be prepared for is Quinn's tears. He gets weepy pretty easily. Dr. Corbin said that's common after a physical trauma, and he's got a lot that he's trying to absorb now that he knows about the amnesia."

She prayed that they would follow the doctor's orders. If they did or said one thing to try to stir his memory or get him to stifle his reactions in that hospital room, she was fully prepared to declare visiting hours over.

It didn't matter that her days of being Quinn's wife were numbered. For the moment, that was exactly what she was, and she would use all the privileges that allowed her at the hospital to do everything she could to help and protect him.

Chapter 14

QUINN WAS THROWN WHEN he woke up and saw Dad and Mom sitting on chairs next to Claire. They had aged too—quite a bit more than Claire had, it seemed.

She gave him a reassuring look and carefully squeezed his good hand as they approached the bed together. Dad and Mom asked him questions about how he was feeling, and he could tell by their hesitation that they were wondering if he knew who they were.

He signaled for the whiteboard. When Claire positioned it and held it for him, he snuck her a wink as he wrote. "Nice to meet you."

He wished Claire could see the shock on Mom's face before she saw his smile. She had been lukewarm on his practical jokes since he was a child, but he couldn't help himself. He and Claire were the rebellious ones in his family, with their inside jokes and ability to express feelings and communicate, and he didn't want his parents to get their hopes up and think he'd changed. He needed the comic relief after his conversation with Claire about children before his nap anyway, and he knew Claire needed it too.

When Claire stifled a giggle and hid her face from Dad and Mom, he felt a rush. Seeing the smile he'd missed so much was worth scaring them.

Claire quickly wiped off the board and gave him a mock chastising look as he started writing again. DAD MOM GOOD TO SEE YOU.

Dad took a step closer to the bed. "It's good to see you with open eyes, son. Your mother and I have been waiting to get the call to come back and visit you. Did Claire tell you we were here every day before you woke up and they banned visitors?"

Quinn nodded. *You don't have to try to take credit, Dad.*

Some things hadn't changed in the time he'd been in the coma. Dad was a good man, but his insecurities could make him look like he was very full of himself. It was Quinn's least favorite quality in him, and he had always fought hard to not react. Knowing that if he looked at Claire he would be tempted to roll his eyes, he looked instead to Mom, who had forgiven him for his earlier joke and stood beaming at him. She carefully put her hand on his arm, and as she smiled at him, he noticed that her eyes were getting misty.

Man, Claire is missing the show! This bed is the best view in the house. He tried to signal to Claire with his eyes to look at Mom so she could see the tears that were about as common as a solar eclipse, but she had missed it.

When the nurse came in to remind his visitors of the time limits the doctor had set, Quinn found himself relieved. It was wonderful to see Dad and Mom and to see that they were okay, but seeing how different they looked made the reality of the lost years hit him hard and exhausted him.

Dad shifted on his feet. He'd always gotten antsy when his unexpressed emotions ran high. "We'll be in the waiting room if you need us."

"Thanks, Dad." His throat was worse after talking earlier when Claire delivered the bad news about their lack of children, but he wanted to acknowledge Dad's attempts at support. "Love you."

Mom moved around to the other side of the bed so she could hold his good hand. "We love you too. We're praying you'll get your memory back soon."

Claire waited for them at the door. He didn't want her to leave. When he tried to write it down, she seemed to know what he was thinking.

"I'm going to walk them to the waiting room, but I'll be back to sit with you for a while."

Relieved, he entertained himself in her absence by trying to stimulate his memory. He focused on the house and tried remembering each detail of every room, hoping that it would be the starting point for getting all of his memories back. Memories of sitting in the back yard eating ice cream at sunset while the early fall breeze cooled them down ushered him back to sleep.

Chapter 15

CLAIRE SPENT THE NEXT three weeks at Quinn's bedside in the step-down unit and then the rehab floor, showing him old pictures and talking about old memories as he tried to regain the more recent ones. His throat was healing and energy improving, so every day it was easier for him to talk. The doctors were finally allowing him to swallow small amounts of thick liquids, and he had grinned like a child when she was finally given permission to bring him chocolate shakes and Boston coolers.

They didn't have much time for the walks down memory lane, because between physical, occupational, and respiratory therapy, his days were full. Getting back to using the leg and arm that had been crushed took just about all of his energy, but he was coming along quickly according to the therapists.

It was just as well that there wasn't much energy left after the therapies to try to stir memories. Bringing up the good times stirred feelings in Claire that she had spent the recent past trying to forget, and every day it became harder to remember that neither the loving man in the hospital bed nor the marriage she was experiencing in that room were real.

Her feelings toward him were as deep and strong as they had ever been, but as long as he didn't remember the hard times that led to them agreeing to divorce, she couldn't allow herself to be fooled into thinking of any of it as real. Someday his memories would probably come back, and he would remember that he didn't love her anymore. She was dreading getting to more recent times and was glad that Dr. Corbin was still recommending letting the memories come naturally and letting Quinn focus on his physical recovery.

She'd carefully pivoted away from some of Quinn's direct questions about the past five years and changed the password on her phone so he couldn't open it to try to learn things on his own. Not wanting to remember those years herself, it was an easy task.

Claire was starting to wonder if it was possible that he would never regain his memory, and she was torn. Holding the truth back from him felt awful, but they were enjoying each other and talking again. She didn't think she could endure going back to the reality that had been theirs before the accident.

It was tempting to act as if the rift in their marriage had never happened, but she knew she could never hold back the truth from him. The day was coming when the full story would have to come out.

As Claire neared Quinn's room to wait for him to return from physical therapy, the discharge planning nurse approached her. "Hi Claire. I brought these to help you make a decision about Quinn's rehabilitation options." She handed Claire a small stack of brochures.

"Thank you." She knew that discharge would be coming soon and had started researching facilities. "I hope one of these will have what we're looking for."

The woman gave her a sympathetic look. "I know you're hoping for a facility with minimal drug interventions. I wish I had more options to give you."

Claire glanced down at the brochures. She would look through them, but her hopes weren't high. Most of the places she'd looked into seemed pretty free-wheeling with the opiates, and she was finding the options frustrating so far in her search. She had added that to her extensive prayer list, but so far God hadn't opened any doors that she could see.

Throughout the time Quinn had been in the coma, she had been adamant about not overloading him with painkillers and creating an addiction in him. Before the accident, several family members and friends were involved with getting a treatment center for pain and opiate addiction started near their home in Hideaway, and she was committed to doing everything in her power to prevent Quinn from ever needing such a place. Faith Weston, the director of the center and a former addict herself, had coached Claire on how to approach the medical teams from the beginning. She'd been a life-saving help.

Faith's daughter, Rachel, and Claire's sister, Brianna, had been best friends since childhood, so even though Claire and Faith didn't know each other well, they felt a bit like extended family. Before Quinn got into his accident, he had introduced Brianna to several of the artists he worked with so that she could talk to them about making donations to the silent auction at the fundraiser the center had been organizing, and he had said many times that if something ever happened to him, he would fight against drugs as much as he could.

Walking into Quinn's empty room, she let her frustration out on a sigh. Even with changes in drug laws, it seemed that all of the healthcare providers wanted to give him a narcotic cocktail and worry about the consequences later, when it wouldn't be their problem. It wouldn't be Claire's problem either if he regained his memory and proceeded with the divorce, but she was determined to do anything and everything she could to make sure it also wasn't Quinn's.

She tossed the brochures from the discharge planner into the tote that held the mail she'd brought. As much as she had tried to stay on top of things in the small amount of time she'd spent at home since Quinn's accident, she was falling behind. The house was full of dust, the cat was clingy, and the mail was piling up. If not for Joe and Dad taking turns mowing, her lawn would look like a forest. Since she had to be more careful about not raising questions or suspicions from Quinn, it was getting harder to familiarize herself with his business in the hospital room. She decided to make use of her downtime by digging through the mail and had started putting it in piles on the bed when Dante, the physical therapist, wheeled him into the room.

"How did he do?"

Dante slapped Quinn on his good shoulder and grinned at Claire. "He's my star pupil. He's taking steps like a boss, and pretty soon he'll be able to start using the cane."

Claire gathered up her stacks and moved them to the overbed table so Dante could help Quinn onto the bed.

Once Quinn was comfortable, Dante pulled out some ice packs and placed them around his leg. "Your job for tonight is to rest. No practicing any of the exercises we did and trying to earn extra credit."

"Thanks, Dante." Quinn groaned, then turned his eyes to Claire's stacks. "What's all that?"

"I decided to bring homework to sort while you were with Dante. You must have been quick today."

Quinn grinned proudly and tried to puff out his chest. "You heard him. I'm his star pupil. I'm Teacher's Pet."

She chuckled at his bravado. "As long as you get to walk again, you can call yourself anything you want."

"How about if you come over and sit on the bed next to Teacher's Pet so we can look at those brochures together? Now that I'm not in traction, there's plenty of room for both of us if we squeeze together." He wiggled his eyebrows at her, making her cheeks warm. Even though he was kidding, it had been a long time since he had flirted with her. It felt good to be reminded of what it was like to have him love her and want her near him.

Keep your head straight, Claire. He doesn't remember. "You know there would only be sitting, right? And brochure-browsing?"

"Whatever you say. Just come over here." He dropped his playful gaze and looked at her earnestly. "I'm starting to get used to sleeping alone, and I don't like it."

I've been used to sleeping alone for months, and I don't like it either. She carefully climbed onto the bed next to him, pausing every time he winced. "Sorry."

He put his arm around her and kissed her on the temple. "This is worth how much that hurt. Whose grand idea was it to take a stand against the good pain meds, anyway?"

Tears started to fill her eyes before she caught the twinkle in his. He pulled her closer and whispered, "My Claire, you take such good care of me. I'm just kidding. I'm thankful that you took that stand, and I would have liked to have seen you go toe-to-toe with the doctors when they tried to turn me into a druggie."

She reveled in being in his arms again. It felt so good. So right. When she remembered that things were not as they seemed and that she was keeping a big secret from him, she forced herself to focus on the task at hand. "Brochures?"

"Let's see them."

They all looked the same, and he opened the next one on the stack and sighed. "I guess we just need to pick the least bad option, fight against the drugs, and pray that I don't need a treatment center like the new one you told me about in Hideaway."

Claire tried to hide her disappointment. "I guess so. Let's see what else is in the stacks. There are some new get-well cards for you."

She had filtered out the cards from the artists he had started working with in the past five years and everyone else who was a newer acquaintance to him and read each one she brought to make sure no one accidentally gave him new information. Dr. Corbin had been clear in that directive, and she was doing her best to follow it. There would be plenty of time for him to read those when he regained his memory and knew who the people who sent them were and knew what they were talking about when they shared news.

As they started looking at the cards loved ones had sent, Brianna walked into the room with a huge smile on her face. Taking one look at the two of them on the cramped bed, she chuckled. "You two, always the honey-mooners. I hope you're behaving yourselves."

Quinn squeezed Claire closer. "Unfortunately, yes. What's up, kiddo?"

"I have the greatest news you can imagine."

"Oh?"

Brianna looked like she could barely contain herself as she bobbed up and down in place. "I've been talking to Faith about you, and I convinced her to let you go to the treatment center for rehab."

Claire and Quinn looked at each other, then back at her. Claire was the first to speak. "What? How? He's not addicted to anything."

"Well, their vision was always to expand to offer outpatient rehab services at some point in the future so that some patients could prevent both chronic pain and addiction. Since they have enough space and staff but not enough patients right now, I convinced them to take you on as an inpatient for now, then they can continue on an outpatient basis when the time comes." She almost clapped in glee as Claire and Quinn sat stunned. "Plus, since they are also treating people with addiction to painkillers, there is a therapist on staff. Maybe he can help with the memories."

Quinn looked at Claire with tears in his eyes and a broad smile on his face. "Maybe God did answer our prayer for a rehab place."

"Maybe He did!" She carefully hugged him and kissed him on the cheek, but her thrill at God's obvious intervention was short-lived. It soon turned to panic.

As her own eyes filled, she held onto Quinn and begged God to make him think they were happy tears. Getting his memory back was the best thing for him and she was hopeful for him, but she knew what else it meant. She might have to lose him all over again.

After Brianna left, Claire snuggled closer to Quinn, both savoring the moment and gathering courage to do what she had been dreading since realizing that he had amnesia. *Please, Lord, show me how to tell him, and help him to take the news well. Please save my marriage.*

"Quinn, there's something I need to tell you."

Chapter 16

THOSE ARE WORDS NO one wants to hear.

Claire's expression had turned from surprise and joy to dread, and she had become so still and silent after Brianna left that Quinn thought she had fallen asleep. As much as those words put him on alert, maybe he was finally going to hear the answers he needed.

"You can tell me anything." He stroked her arm in an attempt to soothe her even as he tried to brace himself for whatever was coming.

She propped herself up on her elbow and looked him in the eye. "You know that I want you to get your memory back more than anything, right?"

He felt a knot form in his stomach when he heard the quiver in her voice. "Right . . ."

"Well . . ." She closed her eyes and swallowed hard. "I'm also terrified about you getting it back."

He froze as the knot expanded into his chest. "That's definitely not what I expected to hear. Why?"

"I don't want you to remember the bad stuff from these past few years." She wiped tears away with her finger. "And there's bad stuff."

Her tears and her words hit him like a punch to the gut. "Bad stuff? What kind of bad stuff?"

Claire bit her lip and looked like she was fighting with everything in her to stop the tears. The fear in her eyes made his insides hurt more than any broken bones could. What could she be so afraid of?

He pulled her into his arms again and stroked her back as he spoke softly in her ear. "Do you mean not having kids? We can get through that. As long as we have each other, we can get through anything, right?"

Not only did his words fail to soothe her, but her tears gushed out like a raging river. He held her as tightly as he could comfortably manage while her tears flowed.

He had never seen her cry like that—or had he? Somehow, even though he didn't remember her ever crying so hard, it felt oddly familiar. Maybe he had seen her cry like that over the years he'd lost.

It was agonizing to reach around her to grab the box of tissues with his still-healing but free arm, but he wasn't about to let her go. He handed her the tissues and held her while she cried in his arms.

"It's going to be okay, Claire. I don't care what other bad stuff there was. We're here now, and it's going to be okay." Maybe if they focused on only the next steps, it would help. There was plenty of time to talk about whatever had her so upset. "Let's go back to Hideaway and break in the new treatment center. At the very least, they can help this banged-up body learn to work again."

She nodded wordlessly. It was unlike her not to have an answer or be able to gather her wits quickly, so he just held her. *Lord, please give her the peace that only You can give.*

Quinn realized as she cried that it looked a lot like the dreams he had been having. Maybe just like the date on the whiteboard, they weren't dreams either. They could very well be memories. As awful as he felt in those dreams, if they were really memories, he didn't want them back.

He kissed her temple. "I don't need to know the bad stuff until I remember. Maybe I never will. Or maybe we can just table the discussion for now and focus on making a new start. Are you okay with that?"

She nodded and burrowed her face into his chest. As much as he hated seeing her upset, at least he was able to be in the position of comforter. He silently thanked God that, unlike in the dreams, she was letting him.

Chapter 17

CLAIRE LET OUT A long, hopeful sigh after hitting *End* on her phone. She had spent over thirty minutes sitting in her car and talking with Faith Weston about the treatment center, and it sounded like it was going to be a good fit for Quinn.

Since the center took an approach that blended conventional and alternative medicine, there would be more treatment options there for Quinn than at any of the facilities in the brochures. There were many benefits to having him closer to home, and Claire was looking forward to having the extra time in her day that nixing the commute to Traverse City would provide.

Since her car had been her confessional, cry room, prayer closet, nap place, and office over the weeks that Quinn had been in the hospital, it was a good, private place to ask Faith all the questions she needed to ask while he was in occupational therapy. She rushed to his room to share the good news.

He was just getting wheeled back to his room as she approached, so she took over. She was getting better at helping him in and out of bed and wanted to practice so that when he left the hospital, she would be fully ready to assist him. After their talk a couple of days ago, she felt less fear and dread when she saw him. If he started to remember something now, at least he had been warned.

She hoped that if he did remember the pain, he would also remember what things had been like over the past weeks since he had woken and wouldn't revert back to the person who was preparing to divorce her before the accident. She was certainly not the person who was preparing to divorce him back then, and she was starting to feel a glimmer of hope that her marriage might be salvageable.

As she guided him and helped him settle in, he gave her his best flirty smile. "Are you going to join me on my bed today, Mrs. Millard? I can help you go through the mail again."

She grinned back and carefully got herself situated next to him. "You grimaced less this time. That's a good sign."

"Like I told you, Teacher's Pet."

"I have something better than mail today." She held up the pages of notes she had taken during her phone call. "I just had a long conversation with Faith, and you're all set. They're working with the hospital and the insurance company on the logistics, and we should be able to move you to the center in a couple of days."

Quinn smiled. "Not quite home, but at least it's in Hideaway. I like that."

He started stroking her hair and nuzzling her neck as she read from her notes. It was just like their college days.

She wanted nothing more than to drop the notes, lock his door, and give in to what he was hinting at, but she needed to keep her head about her. The man coming on to her was the one who planned to spend the rest of his life with her five years ago, not the one who had been preparing to divorce her five months ago. "Quinn, this is important. Are you listening?"

He started tracing kisses along her neck. He hadn't forgotten how to get to her. "This is important too. I miss you."

"I miss you too." Truer words had never been spoken. She tried to ignore the way her skin tingled with every kiss he planted and the way her heart yearned for him and what they once had.

Her guard lowered with every touch of his lips. As much as she tried to resist, when he turned her face toward his and kissed her, she dropped her notes and gave in. It felt so good to be in his arms again, to have him kiss her the way he had when he still loved her.

When he tried to pull her closer, he winced and grunted in pain.

She pulled back from him, careful not to jar him too much. "Are you okay?"

"I guess I have to slow down a bit. My broken body isn't quite up to keeping up with you yet." He gingerly laid back in the position he started in, the one that didn't hurt.

"Maybe it's not such a good idea for me to be sitting here next to you." *For more reasons than one.* She tried to pull out of his grasp gently.

"You're not going anywhere." He grimaced, but pulled her close again with his good arm. "Finally getting to do that was worth the pain. I learned my lesson, though, and I promise I'll behave while you tell me more about what's ahead."

It was good that something had broken the kiss, because she was enjoying it way too much. She couldn't let things get out of hand with him while he still didn't know everything that had happened between them. It wouldn't be fair to him. It was also up to her to guard her heart against getting too much hope up yet. The effort to seal her heart off from him as a survival strategy when their marriage broke down had taken months, and it was all coming undone with every moment she spent with him.

She forced her mind back to the task at hand and told him more about the facility they were converting on an old farm property and about the therapies and activities they had in place. The center wasn't fully ready for all they had planned, but it was ready for rehab and could accommodate his needs well. They even had efficiency-type units available on the property with a hospital bed and a bed for a spouse, so she could stay there with him while he was an inpatient. Since the center had just had a soft opening and they were starting slowly, he would be one of their pilot patients.

"It sounds perfect. I guess we're going home to Hideaway."

Chapter 18

THE DRIVE IN THE medical transport vehicle was physically uncomfortable, but Quinn couldn't have been happier to be out of the hospital. "It's beautiful, isn't it? I'll never take trees for granted again."

Claire smiled. "It is. I don't ever want to take anything for granted again."

"Remind me to thank Evan for offering to drive your car to so that you could ride with me." With Evan in Claire's car and Dad and Mom in theirs, they formed their own caravan from Traverse City to Hideaway.

"I will. I'm glad he did that so I could ride with you."

Quinn winked. "And look at the real world with me?" After weeks of only seeing the outside through a hospital room window, he stared in awe at the trees lining the two-lane highway. They were in their full summer glory and covered the hills surrounding the road.

"Exactly."

When the van came over the first hill that allowed a view of Sapphire Lake before the highway led into Lakes End, he let out a happy sigh. "I've missed this view." With its various shades of blues, the large lake seemed to welcome him. Even though Hideaway was still several miles away on the edge of Lake Michigan, he always felt like he was almost home the moment he saw Sapphire Lake.

"Every night when I've come to this part of the drive, I've thought of how much you love this view." Her voice caught. "It made me feel like a part of you was with me."

"My Claire, I'm always with you." He took her hand.

She laced their fingers together but kept her face angled toward the window. Was she trying to hide tears? "Good day for water skiing."

If she needed to change the subject, he would go along with it. There would be plenty of time for conversation when they stayed at the treatment center together. "Some day I'm going to be back out there doing that."

"I believe you will." She turned her gaze on him, and though her smile was tight, he was relieved not to see tears. "Only a few more miles."

Only a few more miles to help and our new life.

He wasn't familiar with the area where the treatment center was located on the outskirts of Hideaway. Growing up on the other side of Traverse City and only living in Hideaway since he and Claire had been married, he still had a bit to learn about the farm country that was part of his adopted hometown.

The center itself was located on what was once a large farm, and it looked like they were continuing to use some of the land for growing food and housing chickens and dairy cows. It was strange to see something that he had been somewhat involved with but that looked completely unfamiliar to him.

"I can see why I thought this place was special." He laughed as he squeezed her hand. "That sounds weird, doesn't it?"

She chuckled along with him. "A lot of the things we say lately sound weird. I guess that's what amnesia does to people."

"I guess." He was disappointed as he looked around the grounds. "I was hoping it would look familiar here."

"I don't think you've been here. I think your only involvement was introducing Brianna to your clients and letting her talk to them about donating items to the silent auction."

"That's oddly reassuring." Quinn looked at the mirror to make sure Dad's car was still behind them as the transporter drove around the back of the large old farmhouse that had been converted into the main building of the treatment center. Behind it stood a newer building that reminded him of the quaint old motels that dotted many of the two-lane highways in the area. "The place looks nice. Is this what Joe designed?"

"Yes. He did a great job, didn't he?"

"Help me to remember to compliment him on another job well done."

He counted seven doors that he assumed were all efficiency apartments like the one they would be occupying. The building had been freshly painted a cheery yellow with white trim, and the window boxes filled with flowers made for a welcoming sight.

Grinning, he squeezed Claire's hand one last time. "Honey, we're home."

Quinn grimaced as Claire helped him into his new bed in their tiny temporary home. The smaller casts and braces he had gotten before leaving the hospital made getting around easier, and the pain was improving. Still, every movement still hurt, and the ride from the hospital was harder than he'd expected it to be.

Evan and Dad carried the suitcases and boxes that Claire had brought from home into the apartment while Mom started unpacking. Once he was comfortable, Claire started directing and carrying in boxes too. They all moved like a well-oiled machine in the small space, and he watched from the bed that took up a good portion of it.

As Quinn watched Claire make their temporary living quarters comfortable and homey, he thought about how thankful he was to have her. He couldn't imagine anyone else taking care of him as she had or sticking by him the way she did. It bothered him that he didn't remember the past five years, but if things between them had gotten as bad as she hinted at, he didn't want to.

Just how bad had things gotten between them? No one in the family had said anything or given any clue, and he and Claire had agreed to table the discussion until later. Claire wasn't one to exaggerate, so if she said things were bad, they were. Scenes from the dreams-which-might-be-memories came to mind, but he pushed them away. *Later.*

By the time they were settled, he had slept through Dad, Mom, and Evan leaving but had woken up in time to be re-introduced to Faith Weston, the director. He was encouraged when he saw how well she moved despite her own history of a body broken in an accident.

She reached out to shake his good hand. "Quinn, I know you don't remember me, but it's good to see you. I'm glad you're getting settled in, and I'm looking forward to having you here."

"Thank you. I'm looking forward to seeing what's involved in an opiate-free treatment program." He felt comfortable with her and wanted to be honest in an effort to get his treatment off to a good start. "I'm a little afraid to get my hopes too high. I want to be realistic."

"I understand." She sat on one of the chairs that Claire brought from the small kitchen table. "When I walked through the door of the program that this one is modeled after, I felt like it was my last hope. All I allowed myself to consider was the possibility of getting a little bit of relief from the pain, but they helped me to wean off the narcotics and fully get back on my feet. That place gave me my life back, and I'm hoping this one will do the same for others." Her eyes seemed to sparkle when she spoke of hope, and seeing it fed Quinn's.

"You were in a car accident, too, right?" He had heard that she had broken her back in her accident, and the chronic pain it caused led to years of addiction to painkillers.

"I was. From what Claire has told me, you had as many broken bones and surgeries as I did."

He winced in sympathy. "Sorry to hear that."

"Thanks. I lost twenty-three years of my life thanks to that wreck, but God gave me another chance. Now I get to help others avoid all that loss." Her smile grew again. "Being able to do it with my husband and daughter at my side and in my hometown is the extra bonus."

Claire set a picture frame on the dresser and stood at the end of Quinn's bed. "Well, God definitely answered our prayers when we found out he could come here for rehab. We couldn't believe it when Brianna told us."

"If you could have seen the sales pitch she gave to my husband and me." Faith chuckled and shook her head. "I don't have to tell you how passionate and persuasive Brianna is."

Quinn laughed. "Like a dog with a bone. I don't know what we would have done without her convincing you."

Claire shuddered. "I can't even imagine."

"She and Shelby are the best friends I could have hoped Rachel would have, and I would do just about anything for them. Brianna was determined to help you avoid what I went through, and Rick and I wanted to help if it was at all possible."

Just then, they heard a soft knock on the door, and Claire opened it to find Shelby Montaugh there with a bright smile, a glass jar full of fresh lavender, and a fist full of brochures. She was the activity therapist at the center and was there on official business.

Claire hugged her tightly when she came in. "Your timing couldn't be more perfect. We were just talking about you and Brianna and Rachel."

"Now here's someone I remember." Quinn put his arms out for a hug. "It's good to see you, Shelby."

When she walked over to hug him, he was glad to see that she had the same bubbly demeanor she had when he met her as a giggling preteen. "You too! I'm so happy that we were able to take you here."

"Last time I remember seeing you, you and Brianna were in college. I may need a minute to adjust to seeing little Shelby as the grown woman and professional you've become."

"That's okay." Her giggle hadn't changed a bit. "I'm sure this is all pretty strange for you. I've got some great stuff planned for you while you're here, but don't worry. Part of my job is to make sure you don't try to do too much."

"Mine too." Claire squeezed his hand and sat on the edge of the bed so Shelby could sit on the other chair.

Faith stood. "Speaking of that, I don't want to tire you out on your first day. I just wanted to personally welcome you. I'll let Shelby explain what will be happening over the next couple of days. If you have any questions, Claire has my number."

"Thanks, Faith. It was good to meet you again."

When she left, Shelby gave him his schedule for the next few days. He would be meeting the nurse, occupational therapist, physical therapist, and the medical director in the morning. The massage therapist and acupuncturist would be coming in a couple of days so that he wouldn't be overwhelmed by appointments.

He was ready to get started on his new path of recovery, and he was sure this was the place for it. More importantly, he was ready to get started on his new life with Claire.

Chapter 19

CLAIRE FINALLY STARTED FEELING settled in at their temporary home after being there for a week. Since they would be staying there for a minimum of five more, she tried to make it feel like theirs with a few things she had brought from home that Quinn liked and would remember. He had asked her to bring some of their old photos, including one that their friend Lance had taken of them at their wedding when they thought no one was looking. Hopefully, familiar things would help with his memory. She had even brought their old favorite coffee mugs that were a wedding present so that they could start the day with something that felt like home in their hands.

Since she was staying on the property with him and didn't have to commute back and forth to the hospital, she met with Brianna and continued learning about Quinn's business in the apartment while he was in the main building getting his treatments. It was helpful that he was out of the room more than he had been in the hospital so he couldn't see what she was doing or ask questions that she couldn't answer.

He still had no idea that he had changed careers, or that she had either, and she had been able to steer him away from work talk so far. It was one thing for him to think that his father and brother were taking care of things at his father's car dealership. If he knew there was a business that he was responsible for, he would be trying to work on it and would feel bad about not carrying his share of the load.

Thankfully, Brianna had done a great job of figuring out the ins and outs of the business with the help of their accountant sister-in-law, Emily, and Quinn's technology consultant and friend, John. It had taken a village to figure things out, but everything was running smoothly enough that Quinn could heal and Claire could help him.

While taking some time at home catching up on a bit of the housework and reacquainting herself with the cat, Claire glanced at the clock. Time had slipped away from her, and Quinn was certainly back from therapy.

She grabbed her keys and hoped he wasn't trying to snoop in her computer again to stimulate memories. As she raced back to the apartment, she realized just how tense and paranoid she was getting about him finding things out the wrong way.

Being in such close quarters was wearing on both of them, and they were both getting irritable at times. Though she tried, she wasn't able to get the sense of calm she longed for during the quick drive back to the treatment center.

When she walked into the apartment and saw Quinn practicing getting around with his cane, her heart dropped. He was struggling and unsteady, his lips pressed together in frustration. She dropped her tote bag and the laundry basket she was carrying and rushed over to his side to spot him.

In her panic, her words came out much harsher than she intended. "Quinn, what are you doing? You're not supposed to be doing that alone!"

"Excuse me, *Mother*. I'm supposed to be doing my exercises and don't need you chastising me." His sharp answer cut her to the quick.

"I'm not chastising you. I'm—"

"I'm not a child, Claire." His glare met hers.

You ungrateful—oh! She bit her lip to stop herself from making it worse. *Don't say it. Don't even think it.*

Squeezing her eyes shut to stop the angry, hurt tears from springing up didn't work. It felt like she had been transported back in time to the days when arguing and bickering took up residence in their home.

She held her breath so that she wouldn't snap back and stared at the floor, unsure how to respond. *You've been trying so hard. Don't make it worse.*

She hadn't heard his sarcastic tone or her own shrill one since the accident, and hadn't missed either. Silence seemed to be the smart move, so she quietly walked over to the spilled laundry and started putting it back into the basket to give herself both something to do and a way to hide her tears while she licked her wounds.

"I'm sorry, Claire."

What? The words and gentle tone seemed to fertilize her tears. She didn't remember the last time she'd heard an apology after a cutting remark—or offered one herself, for that matter.

"It's okay. I'm sorry too." The hamper gave her cover, and she pretended to look for something in it so she didn't have to look at him. She didn't want him to see the tears that were about to spill out of her eyes despite her attempts to control them.

Quinn started making his way over to her but stopped. When she looked up, he was shaking and looked like he might fall.

Dropping the towel she was folding into the basket, she grabbed the wheelchair and hurried over to him, angling it behind him so he could sit. He fell into the chair with a sigh and hung his head low. Not knowing what he wanted from her at that point, or what she had to give, she silently returned to the laundry.

When she had made the arrangements for them to move onto the treatment center property together, she hadn't given a thought to the tight quarters they were going to be in for at least six weeks. It had made sense at the time for her to be there helping him, but she wondered if she'd made a mistake.

"Claire, I'm sorry. I'm tired and frustrated. Please forgive me." The tears in his eyes showed his contrition, and she walked back over to him and kneeled next to his chair.

"I'm sorry too. I didn't mean to snap at you when I walked through the door. It just scared me to see you walking around alone, and I reacted. I don't want you to get hurt."

"I know."

She put her arms around him and held him for a moment before asking, "Do you feel too tired for a walk outside? Or rather, a ride? These are cramped quarters, and maybe some fresh air would do us both some good."

"I would love that." He took her hand and looked into her eyes. "Thank you for everything you do for me."

"I'm happy to do anything I can for you." She squeezed his hand before taking her place at the back of the wheelchair.

They couldn't go far, but she pushed him along the paved areas of the property. Silence enveloped them and she got lost in thought. She asked God to help her find a way to respond to him instead of turning inward and shutting him out. If their marriage was going to have a chance, they couldn't go back to what they had done—or what they had become—before.

When they got back to the apartment and she positioned his chair so that he could look out at the cows grazing on the grass in the distance, Claire went inside. Fighting the urge to stay there and take some time alone to get her bearings, she took out a chair and two bottles of water so they could sit together and enjoy the warm August evening. Even if she didn't know what to say, sitting there with him was a better option than finding an excuse to hide. That was part of what got them into such trouble before.

They sat together and stared at the animals for a good ten minutes, both lost in thought. At least she was.

"Claire?"

"Yes?"

"The sniping between us earlier . . . is that what it was like? When things got bad?"

"That's what it was like before things got worse."

His brows furrowed in confusion. "Worse?"

"It was worse when we stopped talking altogether."

Chapter 20

OVER THE NEXT WEEK, Quinn continued adding to his treatment regimen and tried to be on his best behavior with Claire. When he was at the hospital and she was going home at night, he could hide his bad moods and frustrations from her to a certain degree. Now they were sharing a tiny space and were always on top of each other—and not in the good way.

Not sharing the intimacy that was once such a strong part of their marriage was not helping his frustration either, but he knew she was afraid he wasn't ready for anything more physical than hugs and hand-holding. Even though he was sure he would be okay as long as they were careful, he didn't want to push anything that might make his already-overwhelmed wife more worried about him.

He pulled out all of the old mental tricks he'd used to keep his desires in check when he was single. They didn't work as well as they had back then, but back when he was single he never shared a small space with a wife he loved and wanted and used to share a bed with.

On Sunday morning, Quinn woke up to sunlight streaming on his face and the smell and sound of bacon cooking across the room. Claire really did know how to put a smile on his face. The staff had given recommendations for an anti-inflammatory diet to help with the pain and healing, and she had gone to a few local places for fresh vegetables along with pastured meats and eggs. They were in eating heaven, and Claire seemed to enjoy stretching her culinary skills.

"That smells like bacon used to smell."

"That's because this pig got to live in a pasture and eat what pigs used to eat." Claire turned and smiled. "Since you have the day off from all of your therapies, we're going to have a special day today, starting with a tasty breakfast."

"I'm so happy that bacon is a health food now." He showed off his new skill of getting himself from the bed to the wheelchair and into the bathroom without assistance. Getting the cast removed from his arm and trading the leg cast for a thinner brace had given him a new level of mobility as well as much less weight to lug around. He could have used the cane, but since it took more energy to use it than the wheelchair, he decided to save that for later. They were going to be leaving the property of the treatment center together for the first time since their arrival, so he didn't want to be too tired or get cranky.

They made a list of some of the places they wanted to visit while they enjoyed their breakfast. He chuckled as he watched it grow. "Maybe we need to pare this down a bit."

"Definitely. Today we're just going to go to places we can enjoy from the car. I don't want to wear you out too much, but I do want you to be able to get away from here for a while."

He pulled her hand to his lips and kissed it. "You take such good care of me."

Chapter 21

CLAIRE STARTED THEIR EXCURSION at Hideaway Beach, where they were pleasantly surprised to find both body surfers and kite boarders taking advantage of the big August waves on Lake Michigan.

Quinn stared at them in awe. "Someday we're going to be out there again. How long has it been since we got pummeled in those waves?"

"It's been a while." She caught herself before she said more. "When do you remember being here?"

"Sorry, sometimes I forget that I'm not supposed to ask questions like that."

"I know." She smiled at him. "Sometimes I forget that I'm not supposed to answer. We accidentally smuggled a lot of sand from this place in our bathing suits and ears over the years, didn't we?"

He laughed. "Buckets worth. Maybe by next summer we'll be able to do it again."

"I hope so." The thought of being anywhere with him in the future sent a warmth through her. "Are you getting hungry? Maybe we should head back."

"Let's stay—please? I'm not tired, and this is great being out here. It feels a little like I'm back to my life." With his pleading eyes, he almost looked like a child.

She chuckled at his antics. "Okay, how about if we run over to the Fresh Green Café and get some takeout? We can either come back here or go over to Shadow Hills and watch the waves from over there."

He contemplated for a minute before grinning. "Shadow Hills."

"Shadow Hills it is." Having multiple options for viewing the big lake was one of her favorite benefits of living where they did.

After picking up their lunch, she drove around the bay that formed one side of Hideaway and over to their favorite lookout over Lake Michigan. Sitting atop the high hill was a great place to watch the waves below and reminisce more while they ate.

Claire wanted to ask if it was sparking any memories, but she didn't want to put a damper on his day if it wasn't. He seemed to be enjoying himself, and it was wonderful to be spending time with him somewhere other than a cramped room.

His eyelids started drooping and he looked tired after sitting there for an hour, so she ignored his protests and headed back to the apartment at the treatment center. When he settled himself on the bed, he made a show of leaving a space for her to join him.

"Care to join me for a nap?"

"I would love to."

It was wonderful to wake up in Quinn's arms even though there wasn't much room in the hospital bed. Or maybe *because* there wasn't much room. It had been years since they'd napped together, and Claire smiled as she remembered all the lazy Sunday afternoons they had spent curled together on her couch during their college days.

When she opened her eyes, he was watching her and grinning. Without thinking, she reached up and stroked his cheek. By the time she realized what she'd started, it was too late. She was lost in his kiss again.

A knock on the door broke the moment. She got up to answer it, both disappointed and relieved by the interruption. Bev had sent a care package with some old pictures she had found, along with some cookies that looked delicious but didn't go along with the anti-inflammatory diet they were trying hard to follow. Claire set them aside, knowing that Brianna would be happy to eat them next time she came to work on the business.

Quinn patted the bed beside him, inviting her to rejoin him. She grabbed the pictures from the box to have something to focus on. She needed them if they were going to be sitting so close together. When she sat on the bed, he took the pictures from her hand, set them on the table, and pulled her back into his embrace all in one smooth motion.

It took everything in her to resist his attempts to pick back up where they were before the interruption. The last thing she wanted to do was stop, but she knew she had to.

She craned her neck so she could look into his eyes. "I'm trying to do what's best for you. If I'm going to be here with you, it has to be just for pictures."

His voice was gruff as he started nuzzling her neck. "I'm not going to break if we do this, you know."

But I might.

She couldn't stop the tears that formed in her eyes. "Quinn, I can't lose you again."

As he held her tightly, he whispered, "You'll never lose me."

But I did once. And I might again if you remember what changed in you. She leaned back to create distance and gather her determination. "Then let's not rush things so we can make sure that doesn't happen."

He looked hurt and confused, but she held her resolve to do what was best for him and their marriage. She reached over him and picked the pictures back up from the table. Looking intently at him, she took his hand. "You know I love you and I'm trying to do what's best for you—for us—right?"

He squeezed her hand and kissed it. "I know. I just don't have to like anything that keeps me from you."

"I'm right here, Q." *And I'll stay as long as you'll have me.*

Chapter 22

QUINN GRUNTED WHEN THE muscle in his hand spasmed. Knowing that he was going to get a "you asked for it" look from Trista, the occupational therapist, he stared at his hand while she started digging into it with her thumb to relax the muscle.

"This isn't a sprint, Quinn. Slow and steady wins the race, remember?"

That was easy for her to say. He had a life to get back to. "Yeah, yeah."

"Why are you trying to push things all of a sudden? You've been acting as if there's some kind of deadline to treatment all week." Having little luck with her thumb, she picked up her infrared light massager and held it to his hand.

"Sorry. I'm just ready to get back to life outside of a medical facility."

Her frown held a mixture of command and compassion. "I appreciate the effort, but you're making it harder on yourself. Once this loosens up, you're done for the day. You need to go home and get some rest."

"I'm fine."

"I decide that." She gave one last deep push into the muscle. "You're done. Go rest."

He had spent the week since Claire had turned him down working as hard as he could in physical and occupational therapy. He was trying to show her—and himself—that he was getting back to health again, that he was a man again and not just a hospital patient. Having his wife see him as an invalid was taking a toll on him, and rest was the last thing on his mind.

When he got back to the apartment, Claire was chopping vegetables. She looked at the clock, then back at him with a quizzical look. "What are you doing here so early? Everything okay?"

"I got suspended."

"What do you mean, suspended?"

He slumped his shoulders and sighed dramatically. "Trista kicked me out of OT."

A laugh escaped her lips, which she quickly covered with her hand. "Exactly how does one get kicked out of OT?"

"By working hard, apparently. I got a muscle spasm, and she said it was because I was working too hard and trying to rush healing. Told me to come home and rest." He made an exaggerated frown and stuck his tongue out. "Blah."

She put down her knife and hugged him. "I'm sorry, honey. I've never heard of anyone getting into trouble for being an overachiever before." It seemed she couldn't stifle her giggle over his predicament, and he joined her as he thought about the silliness of it all.

Just when he was enjoying having her in his arms, she pulled away and turned back to her chopping. "Why don't you relax while I finish up here? I don't want you to get into trouble, and despite Trista's disguise as a cute little thing with that blonde ponytail, she's tough as nails. She'll tell the other therapists on you, and you'll really be busted."

"Fine. I'll sit down and relax, but only if you'll come and sit with me."

"I wish I could, but I have to run to the store for one thing while the chicken is cooking."

Shot down again.

He sat on the loveseat and studied her while she covered the chicken with the chopped vegetables, put it in the oven, and ran out the door. For the life of him, he couldn't figure out what was going on with her.

She had been affectionate and loving since she had turned him down last week, but she was making it clear by her actions that she wasn't taking any risks of something physical happening between them. They had sat together on the loveseat while they watched movies and looked through more old pictures together, but she seemed to find every excuse to get away if he made a move toward her. He knew she hadn't lost her feelings or desire for him by the way she had responded the times they had kissed and the way she treated him. Something just didn't make sense.

He felt like he was missing a vital piece of information. She could see his physical progress, and they were spending time talking and laughing and enjoying each other like they always had. The one thing that was different and felt strange to him was how much physical contact they had—or rather, didn't have.

They had always held hands and hugged and sat touching each other, but she was being cagey even about that. He wondered if her comment that things had gotten bad between them was an extreme understatement, but every time he tried to bring the conversation up, she brushed it off or reminded him they were tabling that topic until later.

Whatever had happened had obviously left some serious damage to her. Quinn made a decision as he sat there alone, lonely, and bored. No matter what it took, he was going to woo her back and get their marriage on the solid footing he remembered.

He picked up a picture taken when they first met. They were in the library with a few people from their English class, sitting closer than any of the others and looking deliriously happy. It had been easy then, partly because unbeknownst to him, she kept putting herself in his path. He'd thanked God when the girl he had noticed on the first day of English 201 happened to sit next to him and ask about an assignment. When they found out they shared the same faith and lived less than an hour from each other, he had inwardly given himself a high five. He thought it was God's intervention when she said she was having car trouble right before Thanksgiving break and needed a ride home, but after they started dating she admitted that the car was fine and it was a ploy to get to spend time with him.

Remembering those days and how easy and natural everything was for them brought a smile back to his face. They had become friends quickly and a couple even more so. Neither gave the time of day to anyone else from the moment he asked her out, and they spent all of their time together. They married five months after college graduation and from that time lived in their own private world. Truth be told, they were each other's worlds.

Lately, instead of putting herself in his path, she seemed determined to keep some distance between them. He vowed to do whatever was necessary to break down the wall that she had built up and win her back.

Now that he was getting back more of his strength and was getting relief from the pain, he was itching to get other parts of life back in order as well. No one would talk to him about his job at the dealership or about the men's group he was involved in, and that didn't sit right with him. They just told him not to worry about anything and that everything was being taken care of. Claire wouldn't even talk about the website they'd started shortly before they moved that sold arts and crafts from local creators, other than to say it was being taken care of and doing fine. He understood following the neurologist's orders in theory, but since he was living it out and missing pieces of his life, his patience was starting to wane.

He was starting to accept the possibility that he would not regain his memories. If that was the case, he was going to need to find out what had happened over the last five years.

When they had almost finished their dinner, he brought the subject up again, praying that Claire would talk about it this time.

"What's going to happen if I don't remember everything?"

She looked thoughtful as she paused her fork mid-air. "I don't know. I know it's a possibility, but I keep working on the assumption that you're going to remember things at some point."

He hesitated, but had to ask the question that had been nagging at him. "Do you want me to remember everything?"

Her eyes widened, and she frowned at his question. She set her fork on the table and looked into his eyes for a long moment. "No."

"Wow." Even though he suspected that was how she felt, he was surprised by the straight answer.

"I wish I could pick and choose what you would remember." She broke their gaze and stared at her glass as she pushed it around in front of her plate. "If it was up to me, you would remember everything except the pain we caused each other and the details of the accident."

At least she was being direct about that. "Well . . . maybe if I knew something about the pain we caused each other, we could help each other get over it. I want to help you get over it, but if I don't know what happened, I don't know how to do that. I don't know how to fix it."

"Quinn, every day we spend together is helping me get over it." She reached over and grasped his hand.

"I don't like not knowing something that affected us and that is obviously still affecting you. Don't you think it's important for me to know?"

"Of course it is, but I'm not supposed to tell you things you don't remember." Her eyes were full of pain he couldn't heal. "Frankly, I wish I didn't remember either. We said we were making a new start, right? I think we're doing a good job at that. I just don't want to lose focus on getting your health back."

He let out a hard sigh. "Part of getting my health back is getting you back."

She reached up and stroked his cheek as she looked intently into his eyes. "You have me, Q. You always had me, even when you didn't know it."

When I didn't know it? What happened to us?

The sadness came over her face again as she squeezed his hand and stood, taking her dishes from the table. He knew that meant the discussion was over. There was no use in pushing it.

As he watched her clean up from dinner, he stayed at the table and asked God for help. *Lord, show me how to get my marriage back to what it once was. Bring everything into the light, no matter how painful it might be.* As much as he didn't want to know the pain, he needed to know everything if he was going to have a chance to fully restore the marriage he held so dear. *Please heal Claire too—her hurts, fears, all of it. Only You know what she needs. And let me have my memories back so I can feel like a complete person again.*

While he was praying, he saw the scene he'd dreamed before, the one where she was crying and wouldn't let him near her. He was becoming convinced that it was not a dream, but a memory.

Things were very, very bad, weren't they? What happened?

Chapter 23

THE STRAIN OF NOT being able to tell Quinn everything was weighing on Claire. She felt like she was shouldering the burden of five years of painful memories on her own. He was getting frustrated by not having answers, and it was starting to become a sticking point between them. They were making such progress on their new start. She didn't want anything to get in the way of it—especially a misconception that she was less than all-in on it.

While he was getting his acupuncture treatment, she called Dr. Corbin from the apartment to give him an update and ask him how long she had to keep holding back information.

The doctor was kind and compassionate, but held firm. "I understand that this is hard on you, Mrs. Millard. What I've asked of you is more than anyone should have to do, but he still needs a few more weeks. I'm pleased with the progress he's making, and I don't want anything to get in the way of him having as complete a recovery as possible."

"I don't either." She twisted the cross necklace in her fingers, reminding herself that she wasn't alone in this. "Is there anything else I can do to help the memories stir up on their own? We've been looking at old pictures and watching favorite movies and reminiscing, and his memory is perfect for all of it. But it's as if it just stops five years ago."

His gentle tone was reassuring. "Keep doing what you're doing, but let's add in something new."

"Anything. What do you suggest?"

"Is there a place that would have more significance that you can visit, or are there people he had a special connection to that you can see? Repeating anything that had strong emotions tied to it may trigger more memories."

She felt a small burst of hope as an idea formed. "Okay, I do have an idea about something that might help if the doctors here will let me. Can I call you in a week or so if there are no changes?"

"Of course. You can also call me if there are changes. I do like to hear about progress, you know." He chuckled warmly, and she felt her shoulders relax for the first time in days.

When she hung up the phone, she immediately called Dr. Oliver, the medical director of the center. He was in agreement that Quinn's overall progress would be helped if he got more memories back, and he gave permission for Claire to start making arrangements for Quinn to move home and start his term as an intensive outpatient earlier than planned.

She got excited at the thought, but then the familiar twinge in her stomach hit her. If only she could decide what he would remember. She reminded herself that the most important thing to focus on had to be his health and that the marriage was strengthening enough that it had a chance again.

It took almost no time for Quinn's case manager to arrange for a hospital bed to be delivered to their home. Things were happening faster than she expected. Knowing she had very limited time to prepare, she called Joe while she made a list on the back of an envelope.

"Hey, I was just about to call you." Joe had been in touch every day since the accident, keeping up with Quinn's progress and offering prayers and practical help. "How's Quinn doing?"

"Physically, he's coming along. Mentally, he's getting very frustrated at not being able to remember." She put down her pen, forcing herself to stop tapping it on the table.

"Sorry, sis. Anything I can do?"

"Actually, that's why I'm calling. The doctor and I are hoping that being at home will help him remember, and a hospital bed is going to be delivered to our house tomorrow."

"That's great news! How can I help?"

Thank You, Lord, for my amazing family. "Is there any chance that you can meet me there in the morning to clear out anything that's less than five years old and to move some furniture around so that Quinn won't have any barriers?"

"I can go over there in an hour or two if you want."

Her breath caught, but she tried to keep her voice casual. "I've got some things I need to take care of first, so tomorrow will work better for me."

"Okay, if you're sure. I'll bring reinforcements and meet you there. Is ten okay?"

"It's perfect. I'll see you then."

She released the breath she'd been holding. If anyone in the family went to the house before she moved some things around, they would realize that she and Quinn had been sleeping in separate rooms before the accident. They had very deliberately kept everyone in the dark about their troubles, and letting the secret out now would feel like a betrayal of him, especially since he didn't even know yet how deep the marital wounds went.

He still had another few hours of therapy before he was done for the afternoon, so Claire drove home to prepare the house. Moving most of his belongings back into their bedroom took longer than she thought it would, but she managed to move enough things to make it look as if she had moved his things *to* the spare room, not *from* it.

She wished she was moving them back because everything was healed in the marriage and not because she was hiding how bad things had been. She said a quick prayer as she put his clothes back into his dresser drawer that they would never have reason to be moved again. After wrestling Wesley into his carrier and dropping him off at Mom and Dad's house, she headed back to the treatment center.

The next morning while Quinn was in physical therapy, she went over to the house and was joined by Joe, Emily, Brianna, and Brianna's boyfriend, Garrett. The men moved the furniture around to make room for the hospital bed, and the women packed away newer photos and mementos and hid them in Quinn's office above the garage. Claire also hid the key to the downstairs office that they used to use for the website so that he wouldn't see that the room had become hers alone.

After her family left, she sat quietly looking around the living room while she waited for the hospital bed to be delivered. It felt a little like going back in time sitting there looking at the old photos, especially the ones of their happy faces staring back at her.

She picked up the picture from the day they took possession of the house and stroked the faces of the excited and hopeful young couple looking at each other with big grins. Quinn was holding her in his arms and was about to carry her over the threshold when Mom snapped the picture. Their faces and hearts shone with hope for what was to come.

Five years. If only I could have amnesia too.

Chapter 24

A FEW HOURS LATER, Quinn gladly accepted a hug and kiss from Claire when he returned to the apartment. "Wow, that's a nice thing to come home to."

"Does this feel like home to you?"

"Wherever you are feels like home to me." He reached for her hand to pull her in for another kiss, but she was already halfway across the room pouring him a glass of water.

She turned with a smile. It was nice to see the twinkle back in her blue eyes. "I know you've had a long day, but are you up for a special surprise tonight?"

"I'm always up for a special surprise with you."

Claire grinned like she had something up her sleeve. "Good. Why don't you take your nap? When you wake up, I'll take you to it. I just need to run a quick errand while you're asleep."

He had been hoping she would join him for his nap again, but judging by the look on her face, she was firm on her different plan. Exhaustion quickly replaced his disappointment after he got into his hospital bed, and he was asleep within minutes of her leaving.

As promised, Claire was back when he woke up. She helped him into the shower, which revitalized him and made him feel ready for whatever she had planned. When he got out, he saw that she had changed from her yoga pants and t-shirt into a pretty sundress that flowed nicely over her curves. By the time he was dressed, she had her car keys in her hand.

"Are you taking me on another field trip?"

She smiled. "Of sorts. Are you ready?"

"Always."

She helped him get into the car, and he tried to guess where they were going as they drove away from the center. As soon as they turned onto the highway and headed toward town, her mood shifted. Even though she had looked happy earlier, the farther she drove from the treatment center, the more he saw the clouds that had covered her face at times when he was in the hospital.

He stopped paying attention to where she was taking him, preferring to watch her instead while he tried to figure out why she had started looking nervous again. *I thought we were past this.*

Her voice broke into his thoughts. "Does this look familiar?"

He tore his eyes from her to look around and noticed that she had just turned onto their street. "Of course it does—wait, are we going home?"

"I thought you might like to have dinner in your own kitchen tonight, and if you want to move back in, Dr. Oliver said it's okay."

He couldn't believe it. "Really? I thought I had to stay there for a few more weeks. How did you convince him?" She was amazing. Seeing their home with so many of the improvements they'd planned was a double-sided coin. It was yet another reminder that he had lost time, but he was happy to see that they'd been able to do everything they'd wanted to. He couldn't wait to see the inside.

Claire opened her door. "I reminded him that you were the star pupil and Teacher's Pet . . . and that it might help you regain your memory if you were home." It would have been hard to miss the catch in her voice as she ended her sentence before getting out of the car.

So that's what the tension is about.

When she opened his door to help him out, he stayed in his seat, facing forward and making no move toward exiting the car. "If going in there is going to make you afraid of what I'll remember, then we can turn around and go back to the center."

The cloud that covered her face was joined by resolve. "This is what's best for you."

The tears she was trying to blink away when he finally turned toward her were more than he could handle. He wiped them away with his thumbs and took her hands in his. "You're what's best for me. I can't imagine anything better than having dinner in my own home with you, but if there's something in there that's going to mess up what we've got, then I want to leave." They could sell the house and never look back for all he cared. He just wanted his wife back

She took a breath and forced a smile on her face. "I'm sorry, I'm just nervous. Don't pay attention to me."

"Fat chance of that." He gave her a once over, enjoying the blush and the real smile that replaced the forced one. "If you didn't want me to pay attention to you, you shouldn't have worn that dress."

He winked as he squeezed her hands. "All kidding aside, we're in this together, right? New start?"

She leaned forward and gave him a peck on the cheek. "New start."

It felt good to wake up in his own home. He wasn't thrilled about waking up in the guest room, but that was where the hospital bed fit best.

As he lay there studying the changes they'd made in the room, he got a strange feeling, as if it wasn't the first time he'd woken up in there. Maybe it was because Claire had moved some of his belongings in to make it more comfortable for him. He hoped that was it, and he was more determined than ever to continue gaining strength so he didn't need a hospital bed or a separate room. Being at home only served to add fuel to his desire to get his life back.

Chapter 25

CLAIRE WAS GLAD TO be back in the kitchen she'd barely spent time in since she got the phone call about Quinn's accident. While she was pouring coffee into her mug, she got a sudden rush of emotion. It was good to be home.

Quinn had spent a lot of time just looking around the living room as they sat together after dinner last night, and he seemed to be both remembering and noticing what was changed. As far as she could tell, he wasn't recalling any new memories, but maybe they would come as he settled in.

That thought pulled her stomach into a knot. She blinked away the moisture from her eyes. *Quinn getting his memory back is the goal. If you trust God the way you say you do, you need to put your marriage in His hands and trust Him to protect it.*

Quinn had gotten around well as he reacquainted himself with the house, which made her worry that he would push himself too much. When she had helped him into bed last night, he looked downright weary. It was no surprise that he was still asleep.

She heard noise coming from the guest room and hurried to make sure he didn't need help getting out of bed. By the time she got to the room, he was coming through the doorway.

"Do you need help?"

"I've got it." He looked tired, but had a new sparkle in his eye as he leaned toward her to give her a kiss. "Good morning. It's great to be almost home."

"Almost home?"

He pointed back to the hospital bed with his cane. "When I get to ditch the hospital equipment and sleep in my own bed next to you, I'll be all the way home."

The next few days went quickly as Claire got into the routine of taking Quinn to the center after breakfast, then working on his business and the house while he was away. Being back there with him had given her a new burst of energy to brighten up the surroundings and make the home a sanctuary again.

He was making more improvements, and she could see his strength and energy increasing. The decision to move home had been a good one, and it did seem to make a difference for him.

It was a constant struggle to fight the temptation to think that everything was back to normal for their marriage. Things were still far from what they had once been, and they couldn't fully proceed with their new start until he knew everything. She had to fight the fear of the memories that might come up, and every day she reminded herself that even though it was slow, they were making a new start. Despite what they'd gone through before, the marriage had a chance.

Dr. Corbin insisted that she give it a couple more weeks at home before telling Quinn more than he already knew, and she had to admit it was a relief. As heavy as the burden of keeping things from him was, it was less than the dread of telling him everything.

Claire put the finishing touches on the table setting. At Quinn's request, they'd invited Mom and Dad for dinner. He wanted to show them his progress and to thank them for all the hours they had spent at his bedside and keeping her company at the hospital.

"Hello!" The sound of Dad's voice as they walked through the door jolted her.

She rushed to greet them. She was less nervous about having her parents around than his, but she was still on edge. If Bev had a hard time not talking about her dog, Claire could only imagine how much work it would be for Mom to avoid talking about the granddaughter she cherished and that Quinn had no memory of.

When she hugged Dad, he whispered, "Don't worry, honey. Mom and I did everything short of making flash cards to memorize the things we can't talk about with Quinn. We've even been practicing not talking about Lily for the past couple of days."

Some of the tension in her stomach eased. "Thanks, Dad. I appreciate being able to relax about that."

"You're a good wife, Claire. I'm proud of the way you've taken care of Quinn through all of this."

Mom handed Quinn a gift bag after carefully hugging him. "I found some pictures from when you and Claire were dating in college. I hoped that reminiscing over old memories would help to spur new ones."

"Thanks, Sue. That's very sweet of you." He tilted his head toward Claire. "I can't wait to see some of her hairstyles."

Between laughing at their hair and clothing choices and telling old stories, they had a thoroughly enjoyable evening. It was such a pleasure to see Quinn smiling and laughing and telling stories from their younger years.

Claire didn't remember the last time she'd felt so happy, especially in Quinn's presence. It seemed as if they both slipped into their old selves as they spent the evening reminiscing. With his strength and stamina return-ing, he didn't even seem worn out by the visit.

She was on a high when they said goodnight to Mom and Dad. No one had slipped or mentioned anything Quinn wouldn't remember, and they talked about old times that even Claire had forgotten. She and Quinn continued with the old stories as they sat together on the back deck and while she cleaned up the kitchen, and she felt truly relaxed for the first time since before Quinn's accident. Actually, in a few years.

She was drying the last of the dishes in the kitchen when Quinn walked up behind her and put his arms around her waist. "That was a great night. Thank you for arranging it."

She set the bowl and towel down and laced her fingers with his, holding him close and leaning back against his chest. "It was wonderful to see you enjoy yourself like that."

"You too. I've missed hearing your laugh." His breath behind her ear was as uneven as her heartbeat. "I've missed *you*."

"I've missed you too, Q."

He started planting kisses on her neck, and it was as if the years that had passed and painful times they had endured evaporated into thin air. As his lips worked their way from her neck toward hers, her resolve to keep him at a distance disappeared. When he turned her to face him, she melted into his kiss.

Suddenly she couldn't remember why she had been holding back. She knew full well where it was going to lead, but it was worth the risk of heartbreak to have even one more night with him.

Chapter 26

THE NEXT MORNING, QUINN woke up with a grin on his face as he replayed last night in his head. Claire had laughed and relaxed for the first time since he had woken up in the hospital room, and even the little worry crease had taken the night off. Spending the night with her in his arms and waking up in their bed made him feel as if he fully had his marriage and his life back.

Disappointment hit as he reached for her and realized she wasn't in the bed next to him. There was no smell of coffee and no sound of breakfast prep coming from the kitchen. The only thing breaking the silence was his own breathing. After the evening they had just had, the bed and the house seemed even more empty without her in them.

He got up with the help of his cane and considered taking a shower on his own, then thought better of it when he pictured Claire's wrath if he risked getting hurt. At least he could get the coffee going before she got back. Glancing at the clock, he wondered where she could have gone so early in the morning. When she ran errands, she usually did it while he was in therapy, and it was too early to go to the store anyway.

Maybe she had gone running or to pick up breakfast for a special treat. Surely she was in as much of a celebratory mood as he was after all they'd shared last night. He whistled as he loaded up the new coffee pot and turned it on.

After more than an hour passed, he started to get concerned. She never ran for long, and if she had gone to pick up food in the small town, she would have been back in no more than twenty minutes. Since there was no landline and his phone that was destroyed in the accident hadn't been replaced yet, he had no way to contact her.

He opened her computer to send her an email and ask where she was, but she had changed the password so that he wouldn't peek at the pictures to try to force his memories to return. She had been clever this time when she changed it, and none of the words or numbers he tried would unlock it.

It was the first time in the history of passwords that he hadn't been able to figure hers out, and he felt a stab in his gut. A password shouldn't be a big deal, but it felt like a loss that there was something he didn't know about her. He would ask when everything was out in the open about the lost years. Actually, when he knew all he needed to, he would guess it as easily as he always had.

When another hour passed, nervousness crept in. He needed something to do and didn't have any treatments for another couple of hours, so he decided to do the homework the therapist gave him to stimulate his memory.

Dr. Lambert, the psychologist at the center, had suggested he gather up some pictures and write the stories of what was happening at the time. Quinn was instructed to include as much sensory and emotional information as he could remember and to write in as much detail as possible. They had discussed the fact that part of his memory loss could be a psychological coping mechanism called psychogenic amnesia, and after he shared the little Claire had said about their problems, he and the doctor were quite sure of it.

He grabbed the stack of pictures that Sue brought last night and went searching for paper. He hoped they hadn't changed where they kept the scrap paper as he opened the drawer in the antique desk in the living room. Lifting up a folder that sat atop the paper with his still-healing and weak hand, he pulled out a pad.

As he tried to set the folder back into the drawer, he lost his grip and the papers slid out. When he bent down to pick them up, he noticed that the letterhead was from an attorney's office in Grand Rapids. Despite his promises not to snoop to try to force memories, he couldn't help himself when he saw both his and Claire's names with a file number on the cover sheet.

If they needed an attorney for something, why would they go to someone over two hours away? His gut hitched. Something was terribly wrong. Curiosity beat out all concern for promises and doctors' orders, and he lifted the page.

The words blasted across the main document in large, bold letters: Divorce Mediation Agreement.

Divorce mediation?

His head started spinning. He stumbled over to his chair, barely reaching it before the lightheadedness could send him to the floor.

Chapter 27

CLAIRE HAD BEEN SITTING on the beach for three hours by the time she realized what she was doing. She wasn't usually one for losing track of time like that, but then, she also wasn't usually one for being so overcome by guilt.

She couldn't believe how selfish she had been last night. It was such a betrayal to Quinn and to their marriage to let her own desires take over when he didn't know the full truth of the troubles they'd had. It had felt so good to be in his arms and to be with him for no reason other than sharing love and passion with each other again that she had lost all sense of . . . well, everything.

Even the pinks and corals of the sunrise coloring the great lake and the gentle waves lapping at the shore didn't still the unrest in her heart. As she picked up her blanket and water bottle, it hit her that she was doing exactly what she had done when things had gotten hard in her marriage. She was turning in to herself instead of toward Quinn or even God. In all the time she'd been sitting alone on the beach wallowing in guilt and avoiding Quinn, she hadn't spent one second of it praying.

She almost sprinted to her car, wanting to get back home to make things right with Quinn. As she climbed into her seat and started the engine, she tried to make up for lost time with God too.

"Lord, I'm sorry. I did it again. Instead of turning to You and talking to You about this, I wallowed. This didn't help my marriage before, and it won't now. Please help me to walk through that door and have the courage to tell Quinn everything. No matter what happens or what Dr. Corbin says, he needs to know."

The drive home took just a few minutes, but it was enough time to gain the courage she needed to start the conversation with Quinn. When she opened the door, he was sitting in the recliner holding some papers and staring off into space. It looked like he didn't hear her come in, and she hoped he wasn't having one of the migraines that he was still struggling with.

When she approached him and he turned to look at her, she was struck by the tears running down his cheeks and pure anguish in his eyes.

She hurried to his side. "Quinn, what's wr—"

"What is this?" He sounded like he was choking on the words.

She had never seen such pain on his face. When she looked down and saw what papers he was holding, her legs started to buckle under her. She dropped to the couch next to his chair.

No.

"Q, I'm so sorry."

He said nothing, only stared at her.

Fear that she had destroyed the shaky foundation they had been rebuilding rattled her bones. "I swear I was planning to break Dr. Corbin's rule and tell you about this when I got back here today."

"You said things were bad, but how did they get to the point that we both signed a divorce mediation contract?" His mouth twisted as if the words made him sick to say.

While she scrambled to find the words to respond, he continued, his voice breaking. "The Claire I remember never would have signed something like this. Neither would I. *Irreconcilable differences?*"

His hand clutched the document and his voice was strained. "I deserve an explanation."

"I know." She cleared her throat, asking God for something to say. "We . . . things got bad and . . . we turned away from each other. We let things die."

"Come on, Claire. Marriages don't just die. Not marriages like ours. Why did we kill it?"

She could hardly bear to look at the expression on his face. The anguish and confusion had only grown since she had sat down.

She was shaking as she reached out and took his hand in hers. "Do you remember when we were in the hospital and you said that we would get through not having kids?"

He stared at her with furrowed brows but said nothing.

"Well, we didn't."

"What do you mean, we didn't?"

"We just didn't. It broke us."

"I don't . . ." A look of recognition crossed his eyes. "That's why you cried so hard when you told me we didn't have kids."

She nodded. "At first, the infertility brought us together. We talked together and cried together and prayed together. Then the months turned into years, and we started arguing more than talking and stopped praying altogether."

His look told her that wasn't enough. He needed details, and she pushed aside her own pain and forced herself to give them.

"We started hormone shots, which didn't do anything but make me feel crazy and act witchy. You wanted to continue them, but I insisted we stop after several months because of the way they made me feel."

When he started to say something, she held up her hand to silence him. He needed to know everything, even things he hadn't known before, and she needed to tell him before she lost her nerve.

"Those shots made me sick." Despite the knot in her throat, she kept going. "Eventually, they made me feel suicidal. I never told you, because I felt like I was even failing at getting medications that were supposed to help us to have a family."

Memories of the shame she had felt weighed on her. "I felt like I was letting you down in every way." Her tears threatened to overpower her, and he gripped her hand tightly when she had to pause to catch her breath.

It took all of her strength to keep pushing the words out of her mouth. "You threw yourself into work, and I threw myself into internet research on infertility. We went into two separate worlds and lost each other in the process. Eventually, we stopped talking except to bicker or schedule appointments."

His forehead knotted in confusion. "That doesn't sound like us." His voice was as pained as hers.

"I know. It became us though."

"What did we bicker about?"

"Everything. It was mostly about dumb things like how we each loaded the dishwasher." She wanted to block out the memories, but he needed the truth. "Sometimes it was more personal and cruel."

"Personal and cruel?"

She couldn't look at him. Her voice was barely above a whisper. "Arguing about your underwear choices and my inability to relax enough to get pregnant and 'forced sex' couldn't feel anything but personal and cruel."

"*Forced*—"

Her head snapped up at the tone in his voice. His eyes were wide with horror.

"No! I'm sorry—that's what you started calling it when even that was by appointment only and only at times when we were most likely to conceive."

He let out a deep sigh as tears streamed down his face.

"I'm sorry, Quinn. This is too much for you to hear."

He shook his head and kept the grip on her hand as if he was afraid she was going to walk away again. "I need to know all of it. This just sounds like a story about someone else, and I'm trying to take it in."

"It felt that way at the time too." She lowered her head and focused on breathing as she tried to get her equilibrium back.

He was still and quiet for a long moment. "This is what I've been waiting for you to tell me. Keep going—please?"

"Okay." She tried to pick up where she'd left off. "We didn't even sleep in the same room most nights. It was never said out loud, but we both started taking turns falling asleep on the couch. I guess it was just easier that way."

"Did I move into the guest room at some point?"

She could only nod in response as she tried to block the image of his empty dresser drawers and nightstand from her mind.

He shook his head. "I don't understand. It doesn't make sense to me that we got that way."

"It doesn't make sense to me either. It just sort of happened over time. I think neither of us knew what to do with our pain, and we both felt like we were letting the other down. At least I know I did." She forced herself to look him in the eye. "I felt like I was stealing your dreams of fatherhood. When you brought up the idea of divorce—"

His grip on her hand tightened and whole body tensed. "*I* brought up divorce?"

She nodded and looked away, afraid to see if that stimulated a memory. She couldn't watch him remember that he'd stopped loving her.

"And you agreed to it?" Hearing the sting of betrayal in his voice, she couldn't look back at him.

"I went along with it so that you could find someone else to make a family with. I wanted you to be happy."

He sat as still and silent as a statue for what seemed like an eternity. "No wonder you didn't want to tell me."

Neither spoke as they sat together, and she fought the memory of him asking if she wanted a divorce in that very chair. She had spent so many months trying to lock it away from her mind, trying to forget that pain.

"I'm sorry, Claire."

"I am too." She took a shaky breath. He might as well know everything. "I've prayed every day that you wouldn't remember that you stopped loving me."

"I couldn't—" He grasped her hand again. "That's what all this fear has been about?"

"Yes." Her voice was so weak that she didn't know if he heard her. When she looked at him, all she saw were tears—his through hers.

He picked up the papers. "Is this the worst of it?"

"Yes. That's the end result of us turning away from each other and shutting each other out." She stared at the papers. "It's the worst thing I've ever signed in my life. It's our big, dark secret that no one knows."

"No one knows? How is that possible?"

"We made excuses to stay away from people and faked our way through when we had to be around them." She shuddered when she remembered how painful it had been to pretend everything was normal at Joe and Emily's wedding a few weeks before the accident. They had snuck out of the reception as soon as dinner was over, and had gone home to their separate rooms and separate lives.

When he looked at her quizzically, she continued. "We planned to tell our families and friends after we filed."

"We didn't file? We're not divorced?" For the first time in their conversation, she heard good surprise in his voice.

Claire's tears returned. "We were supposed to file the day after your accident."

He looked even more confused by the resurgence of her tears. "Isn't it good news that we didn't file?"

She nodded but paused, not wanting to confess the rest.

You have to tell him.

As she tried to come up with words, he spoke. "There's something else, isn't there? I need to know everything if we're going to go forward, Claire."

She nodded again as she blew her nose.

"Was I unfaithful to you?"

She shook her head. "No, I don't think so."

"Were you unfaithful to me?"

"Never."

"Did you mean it when you said you wanted to start over?"

"Of course. More than anything." Scooting as close to him as she could while still remaining on the couch, she looked into his eyes. "You know last night was real. It was more real than it's been in two years."

"Then why did you leave me this morning?" There was no accusation in his eyes, only pain.

Everything else is out on the table. Just tell him.

She exhaled, forcing herself to hold his gaze and trying to gain strength from him. "I felt guilty letting last night happen without telling you all of this. It felt so good to have you back, to have you look at me and talk to me and touch me the way you used to, to be us again, that I lost sight of the truth." It hurt to swallow as she pushed to continue. "You needed to know everything we've just talked about . . . and the rest . . ."

Sobs took over. She could barely breathe.

He reached out and gently gripped her shoulder while she tried to catch her breath. "I can take it. Tell me the rest."

Get it over with.

Lord, please help me.

She tried to look at him as she spoke, but could only stare at the floor as she began. "One morning I took the day off, and I talked to God for the first time in months. Actually, I yelled at Him for a while, then He settled me down and I talked to Him. I confessed everything I had ever done that had ripped at the fabric of our marriage—every moment of silence and harsh word and cold shoulder—and I asked Him for a miracle." She finally got the courage to look him in the eye again.

He looked at her as if he was missing something. "How is that bad?"

"That was the morning of your accident." She buried her face in her hands as the tears rushed out of her. "It's my fault you almost died and now you're broken."

Chapter 28

"*YOUR FAULT—*" QUINN TRIED to grasp what Claire had just said. He almost had to ask her to repeat herself, because she was crying so hard that her words were practically unintelligible.

His head was spinning. He needed to get up and go to her but was afraid that if he did, he would pass out. The lightheadedness was worse than usual as he tried to understand everything she had just told him.

His voice was a hoarse whisper when he was finally able to speak. "Claire."

She looked up at him through her tears.

"Did you just say that you think the accident and my injuries are your fault?"

Even more tears came out when she nodded before looking away.

Lord, help me to move without passing out. He grabbed his cane and carefully moved from his recliner to the seat next to her on the couch and put his arms around her.

"Claire, if that accident and all the broken bones and surgeries were what was needed to get from that," he pointed to the papers, "to us getting back to being us again, then it's all been worth it."

New tears hit her eyes. "I'm so sorry."

His sweet wife. Despite the tragedy of it all, it was almost funny. He couldn't help but grin sarcastically at her. "Did you just apologize for begging God to give us a miracle and save our marriage?"

She sighed and almost smiled as she buried her face in his shoulder. "It sounds better the way you say it than the way I say it."

He held her closer and turned her chin up with his free hand so he could look into her eyes. "If God walked in here right now and gave me the choice to go back and change that night, I would tell him to give me the accident again. If that's what it took to save our marriage, then it was absolutely worth it. It was a bargain."

"I'm so sorry I didn't tell you all of this before." Her voice was a hoarse whisper. "I didn't mean to deceive you."

"I know you didn't. It's all forgiven. Will you forgive me for this?" He picked up the papers again.

She wiped her tears with a fist full of tissue. "I forgave you for that when I was watching you fight for your life in the ICU."

He couldn't imagine what that had to be like for her, especially since she was alone with their secret. "Claire, I can't fathom what would have possessed me to ask for a divorce, and the fact that I did will torment me forever." He stroked her cheek as he looked into her eyes. "I don't blame you if you doubt me on this, but as God is my witness, I will never leave you. I want to be with you forever."

"So do I."

He leaned over and picked up the papers, then held them with both hands, poised to tear them. "May I?"

She smiled through her tears. "Please."

It felt good to destroy the papers that almost ended his marriage. Despite how much it hurt to grip them tightly with his healing hand, he tore them in half, then halves again.

When she reached out her hand, he gave them to her. She tore them into the smallest pieces she could manage and put them into a pile on the side table. "Good riddance."

He pulled her back into his arms and kissed her temple. "That felt good to do that together. Everything is out in the open now, right?"

She nodded. "Everything."

"Good. Now I need to somehow clear my head before we have to go to the center. Will you sit here with me until then?"

"I'll sit with you forever."

Even though her eyes were bloodshot from crying, they looked clearer than they had since he woke up in that hospital room two months ago. He finally had his marriage back.

Chapter 29

CLAIRE FELT FREER THAN she had in years. She had felt like she was walking on air for the past week since she had come clean with Quinn.

Release from the fears of him either finding out or remembering that he had wanted to leave the marriage put her on a high. The walls she'd put around herself in an attempt to both protect herself and prepare for what she'd seen as the inevitable demise of her marriage crumbled down, too, and she let go of the notion that she had caused his accident.

A celebration was in order. They needed to celebrate Quinn's life and recovery, the miracle their marriage received, and the fresh start they were making together.

She ran errands while he was in therapy and made plans to surprise him with a special dinner. She even splurged and bought some scallops to go with the grass-fed steaks she'd picked up at one of the farms down the road from the treatment center. It was one of Quinn's favorite combos, and along with the fresh green salad and asparagus, it would fit in with the anti-inflammatory diet he was on. There was way too much food for just the two of them, but she wanted to give him a feast, and the leftovers would make a great lunch for the next day or two.

While she was at the market, she ran into Evelyn Glover, an old family friend and one of Claire's favorite people.

"You're glowing today, dear."

Claire grinned. "Quinn's recovery is coming along and we're making some new starts, so I'm planning a little celebration dinner for the two of us."

"Your mother has been keeping the prayer chain updated on his progress, and we're all thrilled." Evelyn's eyes twinkled as she smiled at Claire. "How long have you been married now?"

"Coming up on ten years. Our anniversary is in a few weeks." It was the first time in a long time that she talked about the marriage in future terms and with a smile.

"That's a good time to make new starts. That was about the time that George and I moved here and started fixing our house up to turn it into the bed and breakfast. It was good for the marriage to have something to work toward together." She squeezed Claire's arm. "You two have always seemed very suited for each other."

"Well, thank you. We're working hard to get him fully restored, and we're better than ever now. Now that he's getting stronger, we're building for the future." She blinked away a tear as she thanked God that they had a future again.

"Congratulations. My mother always said that if you can be happy after ten years and a crisis, you'll be happy forever."

Claire smiled at the sweet woman. "I like your mother's theory, and I'll take it. I wouldn't want anyone but him. Speaking of that, I've got to get to the center to pick him up. He's always pretty tired after therapy, and I want him to have time for a nap before our celebration dinner."

"Okay, dear." They hugged tightly. "Give him my love, and enjoy your dinner tonight."

As Claire drove back to the center, she pondered what Evelyn had said. *Ten years and a crisis, huh? What happens if you're happy after ten years and two crises?*

She was so lost in thought that she forgot to stop for flowers for the table. That was probably for the best, because she wouldn't be able to hide them from him. She didn't want anything to spoil her surprise.

This day couldn't get better.

As Claire was turning onto the road that led to the treatment center, her phone rang. She didn't usually answer unfamiliar numbers before Quinn's accident, but since she was fielding calls for him, too, she had gotten into the habit of answering all of them.

"Hello?"

"Hi Claire, it's Lance Barrett."

Claire gasped. "Lance! Wow, talk about a blast from the past! How are you?"

She and Quinn hadn't seen or spoken to him in five or six years and had always felt bad about falling out of touch with him when they settled in different towns and their lives went in different directions. He had been such a great friend to both of them in college that when they were planning their wedding, they had joked about flipping a coin to see who got to have him stand on their side of the aisle.

"I'm doing great!" He sounded the same as the last time they talked, and it was comforting to hear his voice. "You would not believe how hard it was for me to find your phone number."

She chuckled. "Well, I'm glad you did! It's good to hear from you."

Silence came through the line for a moment. "I'm sorry to bother you with this, but I've been trying to contact Quinn for a few months, and he hasn't returned any of my calls or texts. I've been getting a bit concerned and wondered if you would help me out."

"Of course I will. He'll be so excited to hear from you! In fact, we were just talking about you the other day while we were looking at the photo you took of us when we were praying at our wedding. He was talking about how much he missed you and wondering how you were doing."

"He was wondering how I'm doing? Is he okay?"

She eased into telling Lance what happened to Quinn. "Well, that's kind of a complicated question. Compared to the last time we saw you, he's a bit of a mess, but compared to a few months ago, he's great. He was in an awful car accident and spent some time in the hospital. Now we're back home, and I'm just on my way to pick him up from his rehab center."

"You're back home? Together?"

Did she hear surprise in his voice? No, she must be imagining things. "Yes, we stayed on the property of the treatment center for the first few weeks, but I convinced them to let me take him home."

"Wow, that's great news!"

That's definitely surprise. Could he know something? "When did you last talk to him, Lance?"

"Let's see . . . I think it was right after Memorial Day, so it must have been the end of May. We were talking pretty regularly and getting together every couple of weeks, and then all of a sudden he was gone."

Getting tog—"Are you serious? His accident was the weekend after Memorial Day. You two were talking and meeting?" It was a shock to her that Quinn had been talking to one of the men who stood up in their wedding and who they had been so close to in college. How had she not known? It was another painful reminder of just how far apart they'd grown.

"Yes, we had been talking and meeting for a few months before that."

"Wow, I had no idea." She shook her head to stop herself from dwelling on what once was and get back to the present. "He's coming along physically, but he's got amnesia. We're working very carefully on trying to help him regain his memories."

"*Amnesia?*" He sounded as stunned as everyone else had been when she told them.

"Yes, his last memories are from five years ago."

"Five years ago . . . and you're there with him?"

It seemed like Lance was nervous talking about Quinn, and Claire was certain he knew something.

"Lance . . ." She swallowed and gathered courage. "Did he talk to you about us?"

The line went silent again for a moment before he answered. "Yes."

A breath of relief escaped. "How much did he tell you?"

"He, ah . . . told me you were struggling."

It sounded as if he wanted to say more but was unsure. He was a good man and probably didn't want to betray his friend's confidence.

"Did he tell you about the attorney?" She had to know how much Quinn had shared, and she trusted Lance with their secret.

"Yes."

Claire felt tears try to creep up into her eyes and pulled the car over. The relief that someone who knew them knew what they had been going through was overwhelming. "I didn't know you were talking—that he was talking to anyone about what was happening with us. He doesn't remember any of that, and just the other day I had to tell him some of the details of how bad it got between us."

"Wow, that must have been horrible for him to hear."

"It was. I would appreciate your prayers for him. We're making a new start and doing great, but he's having a hard time processing how bad things got." It felt good to have someone to talk to about it. "All I can tell him is my side, but he was devastated when I told him we were on the verge of divorce, especially when I told him it was his idea."

"I'll bet he was. He was devastated when it was happening too."

"He was?" The tears that she had tried to hold back were unleashed and rolled down her cheeks.

He didn't stop loving me? She desperately wanted the answer, but couldn't bring herself to ask the question.

"Claire, can I come up to see you? I think I have information that would help you. Since he doesn't remember, I can tell you both his side of the story."

"Oh, Lance, that would be wonderful!" *Thank You, Lord!* "When can you come?"

"How about tonight? I can rearrange some things. Or I can wait a couple of days if you'd rather."

"If tonight works for you, I'll make it work for us." She wished she could teleport him there instantly. There was no way she would rather wait. "Can you get here in time for dinner? It will be like the old days, but the kitchen is bigger and the food will be much better. I'm just on my way from the market and got way too much food for just the two of us anyway."

"I'll be there in a few hours. If you text me the address, I'll let you know my ETA."

Claire's heart soared. "I can't wait to tell Quinn. He'll be so excited to see you and to get more answers. It's driving him crazy that he can't remember. Our guest room is housing a hospital bed, but would you like me to arrange for you to stay at the B and B you were so enchanted with when you were here for our wedding?"

"The one near the beach? Please!"

"I'll let Evelyn know to expect you."

"Thanks, Claire. I'm looking forward to it."

"Me too."

She had to stay on the side of the road for a moment to gather her wits about her after ending the call. *He talked to Lance about us. We're going to find out his side of things.*

He still loved me.

She called Evelyn to arrange for Lance's stay there as she pulled back onto the road. By the time she got to the center, Quinn was sitting on the front porch waiting. When he saw that she had been crying, his face fell.

"It's okay, honey. These are most definitely good tears. The best ones you can imagine." She helped him into the passenger seat and handed him his cane. "I have big news, and I'll tell you all about it as soon as we get home and you get settled in."

While they drove, he filled her in on what he had done in therapy and what the next steps were to be.

When they got home, he stretched out on their bed while she brought the groceries in from the car. Since the first night they had spent together, he had refused to use the hospital bed, even for an afternoon nap.

She sat on the bed and took his hand. "You're not going to believe it, but when I was on my way to pick you up, I got a phone call from Lance."

His eyebrows shot up. "Lance Barrett?"

She nodded and smiled, still as shocked by it as he was.

"You're kidding! How did that happen? We haven't talked to him in years."

"Well, I just found out that you were talking to him quite regularly before the accident."

"I was?" His forehead wrinkled in dismay. "Another piece of information about my past that I have no recollection of."

"He's driving up tonight to see us."

"Tonight?"

"He said you talked to him about us. We're finally going to hear your side of our story." As her eyes filled with tears again, his did the same.

"Oh, honey. We're finally going to know." He reached out his arms and pulled her near. "We want to know, right?"

She nodded against his chest. "He said you were devastated, and he was thrilled that we were here together."

"Oh, thank God." He kissed the top of her head. "That sounds like a story we need to hear. Maybe he can help us make sense of this."

"Let me just put the groceries away while you rest up." She gave him an extra squeeze and kissed his cheek before standing. "I might even take a nap with you. I'm tired today and want to be fully awake for our visit."

"Hurry back. I sleep better when you're here with me."

Chapter 30

Quinn had tried to sleep, but he had too many questions in his head. Remembering what Mom used to say when he and Evan were younger and couldn't sleep, he told himself that lying there quietly was just as restful. He could lie there all day with Claire sleeping peacefully next to him.

He prayed as he tried to prepare himself for whatever his old friend was going to share. Why would he ask for a divorce if he was devastated by it?

Lord, I need all the courage You're willing to give me.

Part of him wanted to just move forward without knowing, but he knew he needed to know, to understand. Claire needed it too. Even though they were starting fresh, the wounds were still there for her, and it was clear that it had broken her heart when he had asked for the divorce.

He was sure that there was no way he ever would have wanted to walk away from her. The answers Lance had might be painful, but they might be healing too.

When Claire brought Lance into the kitchen, Quinn was at a loss for words. The last time he remembered talking to him was several years ago at another college friend's wedding, but his present-day look with more meat on his bones and less hair was familiar. It was surreal to think that Lance had access to memories within the last several months that were unavailable to him.

He stood and accepted his friend's careful hug. "I'm so glad you're going to be staying the night so we can catch up on the last few years after you catch us up on the last several months." Quinn laughed and shook his head as he said it. "I say a lot of things these days that I never thought I would have reason to say."

Lance held Quinn's chair steady as he sat back down. "I can't imagine what it's got to be like for you. I hope I can help you out."

"Me too. I hope you're hungry. We started dinner a while ago so that we could eat and talk as soon as you got here. I'm chief vegetable chopper and anything else I can do sitting at the table, and she transforms it into a delicious meal." He winked at Claire.

"It was time for him to be put to work now that he can use both hands." She came over and plopped a kiss on his head as she handed him the salad bowl.

"I'm starving and ready to tell you everything I can." Lance walked over to the stove, where Claire had returned. "What can I do to help with dinner?"

"Everything else is ready, so we can eat as soon as Quinn finishes the salad and we put the rest on the table."

He inhaled deeply over the pot on the stove. "It smells delicious. You were right when you said the food would be better than when we were in college. I couldn't eat hot dogs or Ramen noodles for years after we graduated after overloading on them for all that time."

Quinn winced. "Ugh, Ramen noodles. Claire and I kept living on them for about five years after graduation so we could get rid of the student loans.

She was more creative than I was with the ways she doctored them up, but the day we made the last student loan payment, we swore we would never eat them again."

As Claire laughed, Quinn looked up at her. "Please tell me we didn't go back to eating them after my memory goes blank."

"Well . . ."

He looked at her in mock horror. "No . . . please."

After seeing his expression, she laughed harder. "Just kidding. We've been following a Ramen-noodle-free diet since the day we made the last student loan payment."

"Don't scare me like that, woman!" As they all laughed together, it felt like old times.

Lance helped Claire carry the food to the table, and they both insisted that Quinn stay seated to conserve his energy. When they were all seated, Lance looked between them. "May I pray for our meal?"

"Please do."

"Heavenly Father, thank You for bringing the three of us together around this table. Thank You for sparing Quinn's life in that accident and for resurrecting Quinn and Claire's marriage. You bring beauty from ashes, and we're seeing the results of that right here. Please be with us in our conversation tonight and bring out any information and truth that You want my good friends here to know. I am honored and humbled to be able to help out my friends, and I ask Your blessing on our time together and on their marriage. Thank You for this incredible meal before us, and we ask You to use this food to nourish and strengthen us. We lift this meal and this time together to You in Your Son's name. Amen."

"Amen."

They discussed Quinn's physical progress and the extent of the memories he had as they ate their meal. While they ate the fruit Claire had brought out for dessert, Quinn looked at Lance expectantly.

"Are you ready for me to jump in?"

Both Claire and Quinn nodded and listened intently as he told them about getting a message from Quinn several months ago, asking to meet up. Lance was pastoring a church in Grand Rapids, so they met for lunch in small towns between there and Hideaway.

"During the first few lunches, we talked mostly about work and sports. I knew something was on your mind, but you weren't ready to get into it." He took a sip of iced tea. "It took a while, but you finally started talking about the problems you and Claire had been having."

Quinn shifted in his seat, unsure of what was coming.

"By that time you two weren't talking much and you were sure that it was too late. You were angry at God for not letting you have kids and for letting you lose her. You weren't talking to Him for yourself, but you asked me to stand in the gap for you."

Lance turned his gaze toward Claire. "Claire, you need to know the pain I saw in him. He felt responsible for the two of you not conceiving. At one point, he broke down and said that he thought God was punishing him for some unknown past sin. He said he couldn't even look at you, and eventually you weren't looking at him either."

Claire looked down and nodded. "You're right, I wasn't." She looked as tense as he felt.

Quinn held his breath when Lance got to the part of the story where he told him he was going to ask her for a divorce.

Lance looked intently at him. "You didn't want it, and for the record, I tried to talk you out of bringing it up. You told me that you asked Claire if she wanted it because you thought you were making her so unhappy."

Claire's eyes grew wide and filled with tears. She looked as miserable as he felt sitting there hearing about the gulf that had built between them. He reached over and grasped her hand.

Lance took a long drink before addressing him. "You bought the lie that divorcing Claire was an act of love, and you thought you were somehow taking the hit for her spiritually by initiating it and acting like you wanted it. You didn't want her to bear the guilt of a divorce."

Quinn lost his appetite and pushed his plate away. He felt like a dam had broken inside him as tears streamed from his eyes. "I'm so sorry, Claire." He moved his chair closer so that he could hold her.

Her face was as wet with tears as his. "I'm sorry I gave you the impression that being without you would make me happy. I never wanted to be without you."

This was all too much. "Lance, why didn't I fight for my marriage? This is what I don't understand."

"I didn't understand either. I had never seen you give up on anything, least of all Claire. But you were angry and shut down by the time we met up."

A glance at Claire told him that didn't surprise her. What had he become?

Lance met his gaze. "You put on a good front when you made small talk, but you didn't look or act like yourself when you talked about what was going on between the two of you. You had thrown yourself into work, and I guessed that it gave you a sense of control. You blamed yourself for not being able to have kids, and you said that when you initially started spending all of your time at work, you were trying to make money so that you could afford in vitro or adoption."

Quinn was stunned. He looked at Claire. "You didn't mention in vitro or adoption."

She looked as surprised as he was. "We never talked about it."

"It sounds like we probably stopped talking about a lot of things." He rubbed his eyes. The conversation was wearing him out, and he needed a break.

Lance stood and started clearing the dinner plates off the table. "I promised myself I wouldn't stay too long or get you tired out. How about if I take care of the dishes and head over to the B and B?"

Claire started to get up. "You don't have to worry about that, Lance. You're our guest."

He put his hand out to stop her. "Guest status expires after the first hour, remember? I'm still family even if I haven't seen you in a long time, and I'm cleaning up. You relax with him." He set the plates on the counter and came back for more. "The two of you have a lot to absorb. I'll finish this and come back in the morning. We can talk more then if you want."

Claire walked over and hugged him tightly. "Thank you, Lance. We needed to hear everything you told us. *I* needed to hear that he didn't stop loving me. I'm so thankful that you called today."

Quinn was feeling lightheaded, so he sat at the table for a while longer. He felt better knowing that he didn't want to leave Claire and that he thought he was doing something to help her, but he was appalled at his own logic in coming to that conclusion.

After Lance left, he and Claire quietly went to bed and held each other in silence for several minutes.

"Claire?"

"Hmm?"

"I'm sorry."

"I know. So am I. I wish there were better words." She propped herself up on her arm to look into his eyes. "I'm just glad to know that your feelings never changed. Mine didn't either. Even when I didn't know how to be around you, I never stopped loving you or wanting to be married to you for a second."

"And you were willing to make a new start with me even though you thought that I had." He pulled her closer. "You're the best wife I could ever hope for. I'll never leave you and if you ever try to leave me, I'll fight it with everything in me."

"I'll never try." When she kissed him, it felt different. It was as if the old Claire was back, the Claire who had no hesitation, no fears, no walls. He hoped she could finally let go of any worry about their future now that they had heard from a reliable source that he never wanted to leave her. He hoped more than anything that their new start was going full steam ahead and that they could leave the past troubles where they belonged.

Chapter 31

CLAIRE WAS SO TIRED that she felt ill when she woke up the next morning. She and Quinn had both slept fitfully during the night, and she had several dreams about the hard times their marriage went through.

Quinn was still sleeping. She held him tightly, reminding herself that they were past the things that had been discussed—and that she had dreamt about—last night. As she held him, she promised both herself and God that she would never allow trouble to build with him again.

Quinn began to stir. When he opened his eyes, it was obvious that he didn't feel any more rested than she did.

She gave him an extra squeeze. "Good morning. You look as tired as I feel."

"You look beautiful." He smiled at her and kissed the end of her nose. "I'm sorry if I woke you up last night. I was having weird dreams. I don't know if I was remembering things or if I was making up stories based on what Lance said. It was pretty awful."

"Were they like the ones you've been having?"

"Some were. Then there were others with random people and events, and you were nowhere to be found."

"Those might be memories too. We were living pretty separate lives." She wondered if he would ever recover the holes in his mind. "You know, we've prayed together and asked God to heal your body and our marriage, but we haven't asked Him to bring your memories back. I didn't want to at first, because I was so afraid that you would remember that you didn't love me anymore. Now that I know that's not going to happen, I'm ready if you are."

"I'm ready. But even if I don't remember any more than the glimpses I've gotten in my dreams, I'm fine with it. I don't care anymore." He captured her gaze. "You're here with me, and we're good. God has healed our marriage, and we're starting fresh. If you'll fill me in on all the rest of the things you haven't told me yet when Dr. Corbin gives the okay, I'll deal with not knowing whatever else is there."

For the first time since the accident, they prayed together for Quinn's memory and promised God that they would accept whatever answers and whatever future He had for them. Claire felt a surge of hope well up within her that she hadn't felt for years as they both said, "Amen."

Lance stayed in town for most of the day, and Claire enjoyed getting caught up with his life over the last few years since they'd spoken. She took him on a tour of the center while Quinn was in physical and massage therapies and introduced him to Faith and Shelby and the others who had been so instrumental to Quinn's recovery.

Lance was intrigued by the work they were doing there and asked so many questions that Claire was sure Faith was going to kick him out.

Rather than kicking him out, Faith gave him her card and told him to call her with all the questions he thought of on his way home.

Because they had a special visitor, they were able to alter Quinn's schedule so that they could spend time with Lance before he had to leave. They picked up lunch at the Fresh Green Café and had a picnic in the car at the beach. Quinn wasn't quite up to walking long distances on the sand yet, and Claire was vigilant about limiting his unnecessary activities on days that he had PT.

Lance couldn't stop talking about the fresh air and the sound of the waves against the shore. "I forgot how amazing this place was. I can see why you two love it here so much."

Quinn agreed. "We think it's as close to perfect as we could find this side of heaven. Once we get the hospital bed out of the spare bedroom, we'll always have a place for you to stay, so come back when you can be here longer."

Claire noticed a look on his face when he referred to the spare room. He looked at her when he continued, even though he was still talking to Lance. "I won't be going back to that room again."

She could only smile and nod in agreement.

Quinn looked quietly out at the lighthouse for a moment before speaking again. "You know, this whole experience has shown me a lot, and it's reminded me how quickly life can change. I want to make the most out of the rest of my life."

Claire had no idea where he was going with that statement as he looked out over the lake.

"Now that I have my wife back and I'm getting my health back, I think I'm ready for a change."

She couldn't guess what he was talking about. "What kind of change?"

He finally turned to her. "Have you heard me ask about my job in the last few weeks?"

"Not at all."

"That's because I haven't thought about it at all. I've thought about you and my men's group and tinkering around with the website we started before we moved into the house, but I haven't given one thought to the dealership." He took a deep breath as he looked at her. "I think it's time to think about a new career."

Claire and Lance shared a look and chuckled. Claire felt a peace about filling him in on more of the details of his life that he was craving. At this point, she would rather ask for forgiveness from the whole medical team than hold more back from Quinn. "Honey, I've got something else to tell you. You already made a career change."

Quinn looked from Claire to Lance and back again. "I did?"

"I may have downplayed how well that 'little website' we started all those years ago is doing. It's your full-time job now."

Chapter 32

QUINN WAS FASCINATED BY what he saw as he looked through his company's website with Claire. She had started telling him more about it after Lance left a couple of days ago, and told him that she and Brianna had been filling in for him while he was getting treatments.

As he read through the information and looked at the pictures of the items available, everything seemed familiar to him in a vague sort of way. "I can't believe I've been doing this full time. This was my dream."

"You made all of this happen." She squeezed his arm and smiled. "You can be very proud of yourself."

He peeled his eyes off the screen and turned to her. "This was our dream, Claire. Was it not quite successful enough to support both of us working on it, or is this another casualty of the marriage?"

Her eyes lowered. "By the time it was bringing in enough to support both of us, it was too painful for us to be in the same room together. Since it was also too painful for me to spend every day in a room full of other people's children, I took the administrator job instead of joining you on this."

"What about now? You've already been doing the work. Do you feel ready to jump back into this with me?"

The corners of her mouth turned up. "I've actually been thinking about that. My leave is running out, and it's time for me to let them know if I'm coming back. You still need me both at home and work, so maybe this should be part of the new start too." She met the grin that had started forming on his lips.

"Partners. I love it."

"Me too." She leaned over and hugged him. "We're really doing this?"

"Let's do it! We started this thing together and we should continue it together."

He looked back at the screen, and a picture caught his eye that reminded him of a place in one of his dreams. "Do you suppose some of those dreams I've had with random people and events are memories of building the company up?"

"It would make sense if they were. Didn't Dr. Lambert say that it might help to write down some of the dreams and see if they became clearer?"

"Yes, and I don't know why I haven't done it. Maybe I'll start tonight now that neither of us needs to be afraid." He turned from the screen. "Can we look at the other pictures in your phone now too? Since Dr. Corbin said you can fill me in on more things, maybe it will help."

"If you're sure you won't get information overload."

He wasn't afraid of information overload. He wanted to know everything. "Since I know the hard information, the rest won't do anything. Let's keep going."

He watched her enter the password into her phone, and it reminded him that there were still things that were unfamiliar. It was going to take time to re-learn, but he was up to the task.

She looked concerned when she turned to look at him. "What's wrong? Did you change your mind about the pictures?"

"No, it's just that seeing the password on the computer and phone and not knowing what they mean reminds me that this time lapse is real. What is 1207 and what is Wesley01?"

"I had to change them to something you didn't remember because we've always guessed each other's passwords." She held up the phone, and he saw a picture of himself sleeping with a black and white kitten curled up on his chest. "This is Wesley, and December seventh was the day you got him for me almost four years ago."

"We have a cat?"

She laughed. "Mostly *you* have a cat. You got him for me, but you're his favorite. He's staying with my parents and getting more spoiled by the day."

He looked closer. Something looked familiar about the cat's one black whisker. "Are there more recent pictures of him?"

She swiped to a recent one of him sprawled in front of the fireplace.

Quinn gasped. He didn't believe what he was seeing. "Claire, he's been in my dreams!"

Quinn looked at the pages of notes he had scribbled when he had thrown himself into writing about his dreams a few days ago. Wesley hadn't left his side since Claire had brought him back home, and he was lying at Quinn's feet purring. Everything about the way he looked, acted, and sounded was exactly as it was in Quinn's dreams, and it motivated him even more to sort out how many of the dreams were memories.

Dr. Lambert had given him a list of questions to ask himself as he remembered things. They covered the who, what, where, when, why, and how, but also any sensory impressions. He found it helpful to look at the questions if he got stuck, and the more he wrote, the more details came to him. As he wrote and remembered, they felt more like memories than dreams. He was finally getting on more solid ground.

Claire was helpful with identifying ones that she was familiar with, as was Lance. She had also gotten his technical consultant, John, on the phone, and he helped too. Quinn remembered him, but as one of the men in his small group, not a business associate. John raved about the great job that Claire and Brianna had done with keeping the company going while Quinn was down, and he encouraged him to take whatever time he needed to get up to speed. Claire, Brianna, and John agreed to start having their conference calls when Quinn was available instead of in treatments so that Quinn could get familiar with that part of his life too.

When his new phone arrived, Quinn felt like a fully-functioning person again. With his new sense of independence, he was ready to start making some plans for the future and could finally arrange a fitting surprise for Claire to celebrate their upcoming tenth anniversary. She had done so much for him over the months since the accident that he wanted to do something special to show her what she and their marriage meant to him.

While he wrote about his memories in the living room, Claire worked in the office, sorting and boxing up the paperwork that needed to go back to the school. Now that she had given notice and they had decided to work on the web business together, they were making preparations to move everything from his office above the garage back down to the main floor where he could access it more easily. He was excited to get back to their original dream to work together, and he hoped that retrieving more memories would clear the way for not only that but the rest of their shared dreams too.

He put the papers away when he heard the knock on the door. Dad and Mom had come for a visit, and he was looking forward to hearing more from them about the missing time and especially about how things played out when he left the car dealership. Claire left her project in the office and ushered them into the living room.

Quinn sat in the recliner as Dad and Mom sat on either end of the couch and Claire pulled up a chair next to his. Wesley jumped up on his lap and curled up as if he had been waiting for Quinn to put the papers away and pay attention to him, and Quinn stroked his back as they all visited.

Quinn was surprised at how forthcoming Dad was as he told his version of Quinn's exit from the dealership. "It was hard on me, son. I built that dealership up with the thought that you and Evan would take it over someday. We still miss having you around, but you loved what you were doing, and we saw pretty quickly that you were doing what you were made for."

When Mom gave him a subtle nod, he cleared his throat and looked sheepishly at Quinn. "I didn't make it easy for you to leave, and I'm kind of glad you don't remember that. It wasn't my finest hour, but your mother told me to shape up and stop pouting. Eventually I did."

Mom patted Dad's knee. "He didn't like it, but he came around. You had to follow your dream, and I even learned how to shop online so that I could shop at your store."

"She learned that a little too well."

They all got a chuckle at that, and Mom started telling stories about the family and expanded it to friends. She got on a roll, and when she started giving updates on the neighbor's grown children, Claire distracted her with talk of lunch.

She really does take good care of me. I'm about storied-out.

After they left, Quinn looked back down at the cat sleeping peacefully on his lap. It was like he looked in the dreams, and it made Quinn think about the little girl who had made several appearances. Claire hadn't mentioned any little girls that they would be close with, but she was still trying to give him information small pieces at a time.

"Claire? Who is the little blonde girl in my dreams?"

She inhaled sharply, then smiled. "That must be Lily. She's our niece—Joe's daughter."

Wow, Joe and Janie have a daughter. He hoped he could meet her soon. No wonder Joe looked so uncomfortable when Quinn had asked about Janie. It must have been hard to keep silent about their daughter.

Claire's face clouded over, and she busied herself with taking the cups Dad and Mom had used to the sink.

He had handled truths well so far, and he was hoping he could get her to tell him the story of the niece he didn't know. Her strong reaction told him there was more to the story.

"Claire?"

She came back in with two fresh glasses of iced green tea and sat down near him. "There are some other things about the family that I haven't told you yet." The shaky breath she took filled him with dread. What else had he missed?

It was devastating to hear that their sister-in-law, Janie, had died while giving birth to Lily three-and-a-half years ago. Quinn had known that it was likely that there were deaths that he didn't remember, but he didn't expect someone so young and seemingly healthy to be a part of the list. When Claire showed him pictures of himself with Lily over the years, there was a strong sense of familiarity, and the pictures fit what he remembered about the dreams. Even though the pictures and stories confirmed what little he did remember, he was disappointed that more memories didn't surface.

Claire took a drink from her glass. "It was awful to lose Janie, and Joe really suffered for a long time. But things turned around for him. He got remarried in May and is very happy."

His mind was still absorbing the loss of Janie, and he couldn't imagine anyone ever taking her place. "Did he marry anyone I would remember?"

Claire shook her head. "Her name is Emily, and she moved here about a year ago. She's a wonderful mother to Lily, and she's been helping with the business too."

"Our business?"

"Yes, she was doing some bookkeeping for you before the accident. She really stepped up and helped Brianna to figure everything out."

"Wow. There's so much to learn." He looked at the faces in the pictures. "Is there a picture of her or their wedding? Maybe she's been in my dreams too."

Claire's breath hitched.

"Honey?"

"I have pictures of the wedding." She scrolled through her phone but set it on her lap. "I know you can handle these pictures, but I'm not sure I can."

"Let's handle them together, then."

"Okay." She handed him the phone.

There were posed pictures of her family at the wedding, but none of the two of them alone. When he zoomed in on their faces in the group shots, he could see the sadness in both of their eyes. "Wow."

"Yeah. Wow. That was just a few weeks before your accident." She turned off the screen and set the phone aside. "We left the reception as early as we could, and I cried myself to sleep. I'm so glad those days are over."

"Me too." He was glad that they were over and more so that he only had fuzzy memories. "So when do I get to meet my niece and new sister-in-law?"

Chapter 33

THE EVENING AT JOE and Emily's new house a few days later felt like a milestone to Claire. Telling Quinn about the changes in the family was the last big hurdle to filling him in on his past. All the other things he didn't know were inconsequential compared to the news about their marriage, the births and deaths of loved ones, the new position she had taken at work, and his career change.

Quinn was instantly smitten with Lily. She had always adored him, so when he sat and had a tea party with her at the kitchen table after dinner, nothing seemed amiss. Claire secretly took a video as Lily patiently reminded Uncle Quinn how tea parties worked and he practiced holding his cup properly with his good hand. Even if they didn't have children of their own, they had Lily and hopefully would have more nieces and nephews to love in the future.

While Joe, Emily, and Claire cleaned up the kitchen, Emily whispered something in Joe's ear, then turned to Claire. "Claire, I want to show you what we did with the bedroom when we moved in."

When they walked into the master bedroom and Emily closed the door behind her, she looked pensive. Changed décor was obviously a ruse.

Claire grew concerned. "Is everything okay?"

"Yes, I just wanted to have some privacy to talk to you about something before we tell the rest of the family."

Claire noticed that Emily held her hand to her stomach as she spoke. She gasped. "Emily, are you pregnant?"

When Emily nodded, Claire hugged her tightly. "Congratulations! Oh, I'm so happy for you!"

She looked relieved. "I was so scared to tell you. I didn't want this to be painful for you."

How could she know? Claire hadn't shared her heartbreak over not having children with anyone in the family. "Why would it be painful?"

"Because I see the way you look at Lily sometimes." She looked at Claire sheepishly. "It's the same look I've had on my face over the years looking at my brother's kids and wishing I had some of my own."

Claire hugged her again. "You're a great sister-in-law—no, you're a great sister. You don't have to worry about me though. I couldn't be happier for you and Joe, and for Lily too."

"I just wanted to be considerate of you with this, just in case, and especially since this baby came along so soon after we got married. On our honeymoon, as a matter of fact."

"It's okay. Quinn and I are going to look into our options when he's back to his full health." She clapped her hands and hugged Emily again. "I'm just so happy that I'm going to have another niece or nephew to spoil!"

A week later, Claire looked into the tote bag one last time before she and Quinn walked out the door. She felt a little emotional thinking about returning to their special spot on Hideaway Beach together for the first time in a few years. The spot, on the edge of the large beach area and easily accessible by a dead-end street with only a short walk on the sand, was one of their favorite places. It was where they had watched their first sunset over Lake Michigan together and was where Quinn had proposed. It was high on his list of places to revisit, and he had begged her to go out there to watch the sunset. As they drove, she asked him again if he was sure he was strong and steady enough on his feet that he could walk on the sand.

"My Claire, my over-protective Claire, I'll be fine." He slapped his legs. "Look at these muscles. They're ready for anything."

She rolled her eyes and laughed. "Okay, but let's stay sort of close to the parking spot just to be on the safe side. We're compromising, right?"

"Right. No running or rolling around on the beach. I'm compromising today. You're the only one I'm compromising with, though, so don't tell anyone I gave in." He opened his car door with the glee of a child. "I can't wait to get on the sand."

It was so wonderful to hear his laugh again and to see his carefree smile back on his face. She had missed them over the years as they had become less and less frequent.

After they got settled on the beach chairs they had brought, Quinn took her hand. "You know, when we got engaged here, we said we were going to come here to celebrate all of our milestones. I never imagined that we would have reason to celebrate a halted divorce or a new start or me regaining the ability to walk, but here we are. I wouldn't wish for anything else."

She felt tears spring up in her eyes. "I wouldn't either. I wouldn't trade one thing, because if anything was different, we wouldn't be sitting here right now." He raised her hand to his lips and kissed it as she continued. "So, what about now? Where do you see us five years from now?"

"Still the planner." He grinned as he looked out at the waves crashing against the shore. "Five years from now I see us sitting on this beach talking about how happy we are and how we hit our new start out of the park.

Whether it's just the two of us or if there are more doesn't even matter. As long as you're here with me in five years, I'll be happy."

His smile still took her breath away. "I will too. Speaking of that, do you have any ideas about celebrating our tenth anniversary? It's coming next week, you know."

Quinn gasped. "It is? Next week?"

"I'm going to give you a pass for forgetting our anniversary since you've forgotten five years." She grinned at him. "What a nice wife you have, huh?"

"I have the best wife in the world. As a matter of fact, I want to marry her again."

"What?" She crinkled her nose at him.

He reached into his pocket and pulled out an envelope. It was heavy stock and felt like an invitation. When she opened it, she saw that it was exactly that. It was an invitation to a private renewal of their vows on that very spot. The date was their tenth anniversary.

Her hand was shaking as she raised it to her mouth. "You remembered."

"Ironic, right?"

She giggled. Her witty husband was back. When she looked up to meet his eyes, she saw that they were full of the same happy tears as hers.

"Forgive me for not getting on one knee, but will you marry me again?"

"I will marry you a million times!"

Chapter 34

QUINN FUMBLED WITH THE buttons on his shirt. "I don't know why I have to get dressed up. Isn't the point of a beach wedding being casual?"

"I think your bride said something about not marrying you again if you showed up in the gym shorts she sees you in every day." Lance helped him with the button on his cuff. His hand was not quite up to the dexterity needed for that yet. "And by the way, khakis are casual. It's a small price to pay for marrying the woman you almost lost again."

"That's for sure." He couldn't help but grin. "I don't know why I feel nervous. It's just you, me, and Claire today, but I'm as nervous as I was the first time I married her."

"It means more this time, because now you know a little bit of what it's like to lose her."

Quinn shuddered. "Never again."

Lance's expression sobered. "Thank you for letting me be part of this today, Quinn. I couldn't be happier for the two of you."

"We both decided we only wanted you there today. You were the only one either of us confided in and are still the only one who knows what almost happened to our marriage, and it's fitting for you to be there with us. Plus, what good is it to have a friend who is a pastor if you can't use him for a wedding every now and then?" Quinn laughed as he headed for the door. "Let's go. I don't want to give her time to change her mind."

"I don't think that's a possibility."

When they arrived at the beach, Claire was waiting on the sand in a flowing dress with a little shawl wrapped around her shoulders. Thankfully, Michigan was in the midst of a fall warm-up and they didn't have to freeze there. When they got married the first time, they wanted it on the beach, but it was a cold September that year, so they had to move the ceremony inside.

Quinn had promised not to take any chances with his leg, so he had his cane in his hand and ready if he needed it to steady himself. He almost needed it when he looked at her, not because his leg was giving him problems, but because he was taken aback at the sight. She was always beautiful, but as she stood there grinning with the early morning sun's golden rays shining on her, she glowed.

He walked as fast as he could to get to her side. When he took her hands, he felt as much of a jolt as he had at their first wedding.

Lance talked about God's plan for marriage and about His way of working all things together for good. He talked about the blessings in valleys and God's greater plans, and about what he and others had always observed in the special relationship Quinn and Claire shared. When he prayed for a lifetime of love and happiness for them, Quinn felt as if God was there with His arms wrapped around them and blessing their union.

With it being a weekday, Quinn had to get back for OT and Lance had to head back to Grand Rapids to work. Since they had wanted to renew their vows on their actual anniversary, they worked around the calendar as much as they could.

When Claire picked Quinn up after his therapy sessions, she was still wearing her pretty dress and greeted him with a lingering kiss and a smile. When they arrived home, he glanced outside and saw the elegant white cloth, candles, and flowers she had put on the table on the deck.

He looked down at the t-shirt and gym shorts he had worn in therapy. "Do I have to get dressed up again?"

"No, but you can take a shower while I put the finishing touches on dinner if you'd like."

He couldn't wait to get back to her, and he took as fast a shower as he could. Since he was finally able to shower and dress without assistance, he was on his own. Putting his shirt and khakis from the morning wedding back on, he rolled up the sleeves and spared himself the agony of trying to get the buttons on the cuff right. When he got back to the kitchen, he got the desired response to his choice to ditch the therapy clothes.

Claire put her arms around his neck and kissed him as if she had all the time in the world. "You look very handsome, Mr. Millard."

"And you're the most beautiful bride I've ever seen, Mrs. Millard. Even more beautiful than the first time we did this. It makes me want to keep marrying you over and over." The way she kissed him convinced him that she would marry him over and over too.

Dinner looked almost ready. She had prepared a special meal, complete with cold tenderloin salad and champagne flutes filled with the fresh ginger tea she had become so fond of lately.

"Now that I have two working hands for the most part, can I help get the food on the table?"

"Nope." She nudged him toward the door that led outside. "You've had a big day, so you get to just sit down and let me serve you."

"You've been doing so much of that. I owe you a lot of serving once I'm back to full capacity."

"You'll get your chance." She winked as she set his salad in front of him.

They toasted each other and talked over dinner about what they appreciated about each other and their marriage. It was a tradition they had started when they celebrated the first month of marriage over candles and Ramen noodles in their tiny one-bedroom apartment.

Claire reached out and took his hand. "It's nice to get back to our old anniversary tradition."

"Get back?" His heart fell. Of course they would have let that go. "How long has it been?"

"Over the last couple of years we didn't make a big deal out of our anniversary. I think the pain was too much to bear, and we just found excuses not to make a big event out of our anniversary."

He lifted her fingers to his lips and kissed them. "From now on, every anniversary gets celebrated. We almost lost this marriage, so every day that we're together is an even bigger gift."

"That's a great plan." She stood and stacked their plates and hustled them into the house. When she returned, she walked over to the old rocking bench. "Join me?"

"Always."

When he sat down next to her, she handed him a beautifully wrapped box. "Happy anniversary."

"Aww, but I can't go shopping, so I didn't get you anything."

She nudged him. "If I remember correctly, you gave me a perfect and beautiful morning wedding on a beach."

"Well, that's true. This looks fancy though." The rectangular box looked like the kind a watch would come in, but it wasn't heavy enough for that. He noticed that she held her breath while he carefully unwrapped it.

When he pulled the lid off the box, all he saw was the plus sign. He gasped and looked up at her. "Really?"

She nodded as tears fell down her cheeks. "We're pregnant. I guess God did plan to start our family here in this house. He just had different timing than we had."

He pulled her into his arms, thanking God for resurrecting their marriage and growing their family. As they sat there together holding each other as tightly as they ever had, their tears mingled again. This time, they were all tears of joy.

"You're going to be a mom."

"And you're going to be a dad."

He pulled his injured hand away and examined it. "I guess I'd better work harder in OT to get these fingers in working order."

"So that you can change diapers?" She gave him a teasing look.

He shook his head. "Since you did everything short of changing diapers for me, I'll be happy to be the chief diaper changer for this little one. I'm pretty sure I'm already able to do that though."

"Then why do you need to have your fingers back in working order?"

"Right there. See that?" He pointed out to the corner of the yard and grinned. "I've got a sandbox to build."

How long is it going to take for best friends Cynthia Huntley and Wyatt Henry to realize what everyone in town knows ~ that they are in love? Keep reading for a peek of Wyatt and Cynthia's story!

A Note From the Author

I love marital romances, don't you? This particular one went through a dramatic change between the first draft and the final result. In the first version of it, Claire and Quinn weren't from Summit County but had visited previously and loved being there. I was hoping that having 1) a married couple and 2) a couple who didn't have ties to most of the characters readers know wouldn't be a problem. I'll never know, because God had a better idea for Quinn and Claire!

My writing process goes something like this: draft – set aside – edit/revise – set aside – edit – critique partner edit – beta reads – edit/polish – proofreader – release. Does that sound like a mess? It's usually worse! That being said, it usually works for me. Because of those "set aside" times, I'm usually working on more than one book at a time. Another step in that process is reading the others in the series when a book is almost finished to make sure I'm not making the continuity mistakes that drive me crazy as a reader. After finishing the first draft of this book, I read the first four books in preparation for the final polish of Repairing Hearts (book 5). When I read Second Chance (book 1) again, I realized that I had mentioned Joe Callahan's married sister but didn't say anything about her having children like I thought I had. I literally yelled, "Claire can be a Callahan!" The cat looked at me funny, but that's nothing new.

It was so fun to rewrite the story and have Claire and Quinn be part of the Callahan family and the community of Hideaway. I especially liked what they added to Brianna's story.

The seed for this story was the idea of a couple who were on the verge of divorce and for an accident and amnesia to give them a chance to remember how much they loved each other. As I got to know them, I wanted no question that they still loved each other deeply. Instead of having one or both of them toss aside the marriage, there needed to be an outside force that put so much strain on it that they gave up. Working in adoptions for several years, I saw first-hand how hard infertility is on marriages. It either strengthens them or breaks them. That made for a perfect scenario for Quinn and Claire.

Deciding whether or not to have them conceive took some time. There was a great argument for starting their family through adoption, but I just really wanted to give them a pregnancy that came about when they weren't trying but were just expressing their love, desire, and need for each other. I've known so many couples who suddenly conceived after years of trying, and it filled my heart to give that experience to Claire and Quinn.

Now that we've gotten Quinn and Claire back on their feet, it's time to check back in on the Huntley family. In the next book, Cynthia and her best friend, Wyatt, need to wake up to the reality that they are made for each other. They were such a fun couple to write, and Wyatt is the perfect man to help Cynthia hope for a future after enduring abuse in her past. Zack and Laci have big roles in their story too!

If you want to be the first to see a sneak peek of new books and hear about sales as well as see pictures from the real place that looks like Summit County, please subscribe to my newsletter by following the instructions for the QR code on the last page of the book! Newsletters aren't for everyone, so if you would just like to be notified of new releases, you can follow me on Amazon or Bookbub and they'll email you.

Thank you for spending your valuable time with my imaginary friends. If you would like to leave a one or two sentence review on Amazon or Bookbub so that other readers can be introduced to this book, I would be so grateful! They are one of the best ways for readers to find new-to-them authors and books. If leaving a review is just too much (I get it ~ they take precious time that could be spent reading!), but you'd like to leave a rating instead, you can do that too! Thanks for reading!

See you in Summit County,

Katherine

Surprise Love in Summit County

His dangerous job and her abusive past have kept these best friends out of relationships for years. When they can't deny their feelings any longer, it's decision time. Will fear win or will they trust God and give love a chance?

Everyone knows Wyatt and Cynthia are in love and perfect for each other. Everyone except Wyatt and Cynthia. The best friends and neighbors share meals, celebrations, sorrows, and prayers with each other—everything but the feelings they both fight.

He sacrificed marriage and family for a career on the police force. She prevented the risk of exposing herself and her son to another abuser by avoiding men and relationships entirely. Having each other as their permanent plus-one without the risk of love was a comfortable and convenient arrangement . . . until it wasn't.

When they're confronted with the feelings they've refused to acknowledge for years, they can't go back to what they had before. Will they rely on God and each other to face their fears and grasp love?

Surprise Love in Summit County ~ Sneak Peek

Chapter 1

It wasn't quite right. Cynthia Huntley scanned the living room once more, looking for the perfect spot. Putting the *Welcome Home* sign on the mantle seemed anti-climactic, nowhere near the hero's welcome Zachary deserved. She walked outside one more time, certain that she could find a better place for it.

Standing in the middle of the sidewalk with her hands on her hips, she stared at her front porch and visualized where it would catch Zachary's eye without being too flashy. She tilted her head and squinted in concentration as she pictured it hanging over the steps.

"Maybe it needs balloons—no, scratch that. Balloon pops can trigger PTSD reactions." She added streamers to her mental shopping list instead.

Roscoe's wagging tail and quick descent from the front porch, along with the familiar sound of heavy footsteps behind her, let her know that Wyatt had crossed the street and joined her on the lawn. His breath tickled her ear as he whispered, "What are we looking at?"

"The *Welcome Home* sign."

"Looks great."

She elbowed him in the ribs. "Very funny."

He doubled over in one of his standard attempts at hilarity. "Well, it's going to look great when you put it up. I'm just pre-complimenting you on yet another job well done."

"You don't have to kiss up to me, Wyatt. Your dinner is almost ready and I just put the chicken and corn on the grill."

He rubbed his stomach. "Good, I'm starving. Do I have time for my upper-body workout before we eat?"

"Definitely." As she led him into the house and into Zachary's room, she noticed the box he was carrying. "Hey, is that a gift for me?"

"Actually, it sort of is. I got some noise-canceling headphones for Zack. I know he said no gifts at his party, but I thought he might accept one if it was something that would help him."

He was so thoughtful. Zachary would love them. "That's a great gift. They'll come in handy when people start in with Labor Day fireworks in a couple of weeks."

He winked. "And when he wants to listen to Metalopia."

"Yes!" She threw her arms around him. "Wyatt, you did give me a gift!"

"Told you." He set the box on Zachary's dresser and assessed the fabric bolts that were neatly stacked on the bed.

"As much as I'm going to miss having the extra storage space, I can't wait to have Zachary home."

His smile met hers. "I know, and he'll appreciate not having all these girly fabrics in here when he gets home tomorrow." He picked up several of the bolts of fabric and headed to her workroom. "This time will be a whole different homecoming than when he came back from Walter Reed. You finally get to throw a party."

"I'm so excited." She stopped herself from clapping her hands in glee as she followed him. "Thank you again for my new shelves. They're perfect for the fabric."

"You're very welcome. Bottom shelf?"

She chuckled. "It's scary how well you know my organization system. I'm going to go make the salad while you finish up. Don't pull any muscles—we're going to need them for cornhole at the party."

He saluted her as he strode toward Zachary's room for another armful. "What's with all this extra fabric, anyway?"

She answered back as she walked to the kitchen. "Two party dresses, a bridal veil, Fall Festival projects, and a few fabrics that were on sale and begging me to make something out of them. I finished the rest of the alteration orders I had this afternoon."

"Yeah, I've noticed your lights on later than usual."

"I've been too excited to sleep the last couple of days, so I decided to work instead."

He entered the kitchen and pulled the tongs out of the drawer. "Excited or nervous?"

"A little of both, I suppose." Her hands fell still over the salad. "He's sounded so good on the phone since he's been at the Veterans Ranch, but I'm afraid to get my hopes up. PTSD doesn't just go away."

"True, but he's sounded great the last few times I've talked to him, and they wouldn't discharge him if he wasn't ready. Four months is long enough for them to know, right?"

She sure hoped so. Either way, God had Zachary under His wing. "Right. I'm glad he'll be here for a few days before the party so I can see for myself how he's doing. I've already told everyone that if he's struggling, I'm canceling it."

"Good call. I don't think you'll need to though." He headed out the back door to retrieve the chicken and corn from the grill.

By the time Wyatt returned, Cynthia was seated at the table. When he sat and took her hand before saying grace, she was overwhelmed with thankfulness for his presence in her life. "Thank you for everything, Wyatt."

"It was only five minutes of lifting things, Cyn."

Her eyes started to sting. "You know what I mean. That day . . ."

"You've already thanked me for that, and I've already told you there were no thanks needed." His large hand surrounded hers. "I told you I would be here if you and Zack needed me. I'm just sorry you did."

She nodded. "And now he's better, and I get to throw the party I thought might never happen. Did I mention you're in charge of the grill?"

"Cynthia Marie, I'm offended that there would be a question of whether or not I'm manning the grill. Of course I'm in charge of it."

"Okay, Chef. Settle down." She chuckled. "Say grace for us before the food gets cold."

Chapter 2

Sometimes Wyatt Henry hated his job. He exhaled slowly and spoke in a measured tone. "Put the gun down, Gus."

"You first."

"You know that's not how it works." Wyatt studied Gus's hand in his peripheral vision while keeping his eyes trained on his face. "You know I don't want to hurt you."

"If I put mine down, you're just gonna pull out your stupid cuffs." He practically teetered as the words slurred out of his mouth. "I'm not goin' to jail again. I'm not!"

"I'd rather take you to jail than the hospital, Gus—or worse yet, the morgue. Work with me here."

Gus finally looked at him. His eyes were wild with fear.

Wyatt calmly held his gaze. "I know you're scared, Gus." He tilted his head in the direction of Gus's long-suffering girlfriend, shielding herself behind the tattered couch. "So is Maggie."

Maggie spoke through her tears. "Please, Gus. Do what he says. I'll come visit you as soon as they let me." She stretched her hand toward him, pleading.

Again.

Wyatt had to keep his thoughts and focus centered on the teetering man and not the woman who returned to him time after time despite years of drunkenness and threats. This time she wasn't even making a pretense of leaving.

One would think that knowing every law enforcement officer and bail bondsman in the area by name would influence her decisions. Of course, one would think that staring into the barrel of a revolver—again—would too. It was as if she had just accepted nights like this as part of her relationship. Or that she was completely broken.

Wyatt's arm was getting tired, and he hoped Gus's was too. "Gus . . . let's end this peacefully. Put the gun down. Maybe this can be the time that things change for you two." He had been called to the run-down farmhouse too many times to believe a word of that, but he said what he needed to in these situations and hoped that someday change really would happen.

"Please, Gus. I'm sorry, baby." Maggie's voice was barely a squeak.

Gus stared at her with an ever-shifting expression. The fear and anger seemed to be dissipating, and Wyatt prayed that reason would take over—not that reasoning was Gus's strong suit.

After a moment Gus lowered the gun and sighed. "That's all I wanted to hear."

Wyatt bit the inside of his cheek to keep his words to himself and hide his irritation at the man's sense of entitlement and complete lack of self-awareness. He had very little patience for men who took out their anger and insecurities on women, especially ones he had to drag away on a regular basis.

Don't react. Get the job done and get her to safety.

"Good job, Gus. Set the gun on the floor and push it to Officer Brody."

"I know." He rolled his eyes and spat the words. "This is not my first rodeo."

No kidding. I'm getting sick of the bull at this particular one.

Gus finally acquiesced, setting the gun on the worn wood floor and sliding it toward Brody with his foot, all the while glaring at Wyatt. As

Brody cuffed him and walked him out to the car, Wyatt had to block the door to stop Maggie from running after them.

"You know you can't do that, Maggie."

"Can't I just say goodbye?" She tried to lean around Wyatt's large frame.

"You can talk to him tomorrow. Right now you need to let us do our job."

"But he didn't mean it."

"Maggie, look at me." The desperate woman's tears jerked at his heart. "Whether he meant it or not, and whether he's sorry tomorrow or not, he could have killed you. It's my job to try to prevent that from happening."

She stood sobbing as Wyatt reached into his pocket and pulled out the card with the domestic violence hotline number on it and handed it to her. Again.

It was a waste of time and paper giving it to her, but he needed to do something. She probably had the number memorized by now, or at least on speed dial.

"I wish I could do more for you, Maggie." He reached over to the tissue box and handed one to her. "I wish you would let me."

With her, he meant every word. Unfortunately, the only way he could think of to help her was to kidnap her and get her out of the situation long enough to wake up. Last he heard, that was still illegal. "There are people who can help you. The shelter is there, waiting, but it's up to you now. Call them . . . please, Maggie."

She nodded, looking at the floor. "I will. Thank you, Officer Henry."

You'll call, but you won't give the shelter another thought. He wished he had the power to make people stop lying to themselves, but that was far above his pay grade.

As he walked the gravel path to the car, he asked God to give her courage and strength to get out. The love he once had for his job was waning, and situations like the one he'd spent the last hour in wore him out. He needed to schedule a day to get out on Lake Michigan, where the only weapons he needed were lures, rods, and nets, and he needed to do it soon.

He had learned as an MP in the Marines more than twenty years ago that too many domestic calls could wear a person down and that regular R and R was a necessity of the job. It was a toss-up which was worse, a civilian inadequately trained in firearm safety who made a hobby of getting drunk and threatening his girlfriend, or a highly-trained Marine who snapped after too many deployments. Either way, his least favorite call was one that could end with someone getting hurt.

Checking his watch, he was pleasantly surprised that his shift was already over. *Time flies when you're reasoning with armed drunks.*

Brody would take care of processing Gus and it would take Wyatt no time to do the report, so his day was almost over. Too bad there was no copy-and-paste for that. All that ever changed on a domestic disturbance call to Gus's place was the date and time. In a small town like Hideaway, even the names of the arresting officers were usually the same.

His stomach growled and reminded him of the enchiladas Cynthia had promised him. He had been thinking about them since she texted a picture of them earlier, and he was more than ready to indulge. Between her cooking and her company, his day would be getting better soon.

Ebook and paperback available on Amazon!

Acknowledgments

I couldn't write a single sentence if God wasn't behind the scenes whispering to me. I feel like I should expand on that thought, but it's pretty complete. I'm so thankful for the ideas and guidance that He's given in every book and for the way He has used these little stories to touch hearts—both readers' and my own!

Having the support and encouragement of friends and family is a huge gift in life. Having friends and family members who are willing to beta read and discuss story ideas with me ad nauseam is nothing short of amazing!

Speaking of beta readers, they, along with my critique partner, editors, and proofreaders make the process of putting out a book much less daunting. I appreciate every typo spotted, word of encouragement, and honest opinion—especially the answers that lead me to correct mistakes or plot holes! My team makes every book better, and it's impossible to put my appreciation into words. (Plus, it's fun to talk about the books! It's like my own private book club every time.)

My cover designer has transformed the look of this series, and this cover is one of my absolute favorites! He's understood and helped to shape my vision of the series visuals, and he's brought the ideas alive!

I always save my readers for last in this list, because you make this whole thing a blessing I could never have even imagined. Many of you have become friends, and I treasure each and every one of you. Thank you for letting me be a part of your life!

About the Author

Katherine Karrol is both a fan and an author of sweet Christian romance stories. Because she does not possess the ability or desire to put a good book down and generally reads them in one sitting, she writes books that can be read in the same way.

Her books are meant to entertain, encourage, and possibly inspire the reader to take chances, trust God, and laugh in the midst of this thing we call life. The people she interacts with in her professional world have absolutely no idea that she writes these books, so by reading this, you agree to keep her secret.

If you would like to talk about your favorite character, share who you were picturing as you were reading, or just chat about books and pretty places, you can email her at KatherineKarrol@gmail.com or follow her on the usual social media outlets. She's most active on Facebook, where she has a small reader group and loves to talk about books. The next most likely place to see evidence of her existence is Pinterest, where she has boards for all of her books, memes, and other bookish things. She seems to think that Instagram is a place to look at other posts but usually forgets to make her own. Maybe someday she'll get on the ball with that. Maybe.

Books

Summit County Series

Second Chance in Summit County

Trusting Again in Summit County

New Beginnings in Summit County

Taking Risk in Summit County

Repairing Hearts in Summit County

Returning Home in Summit County

Love Remembered in Summit County

Surprise Love in Summit County

Playing Married in Summit County

Hearts of Summit Series

Stay for Love

Open the camera app on your phone and aim it here to get a link to join my email community!

If the QR code is too confusing, just email me for the link :)

Made in United States
Orlando, FL
14 August 2022

21022652R00107